christmas
with the
sheriff

christmas
with the
sheriff

VICTORIA
JAMES

Entangled Publishing, LLC
2614 South Timberline Road
Suite 109
Fort Collins, CO 80525
Visit our website at www.entangledpublishing.com.

Bliss is an imprint of Entangled Publishing, LLC. For more information on our titles, visit http://www.entangledpublishing.com/category/bliss

Edited by Alethea Spiridon
Cover design by Melody Pond
Cover art from iStock

Manufactured in the United States of America

First Edition November 2016

Prologue

Three days ago, Julia Bailey had ceased to exist.

She was no longer a mother, a wife, or anything that mattered.

Biting winds ripped the remaining copper and orange leaves from the looming Quaking Aspens, the rain trampling them, matting them to the soggy grass, plastering them to the tops of umbrellas. Her only shelter from the wind and rain was the large, black umbrella that had appeared over her the moment the service began.

Her mother-in-law touched her arm and Julia turned to look at her for the briefest of moments, before looking down the row at the rest of her in-laws. Michael's family. They were all here, as they would be. Michael's twin brother, Jack, head bent staring into the graves. He hadn't looked at anyone today. The youngest Bailey sibling, Gwen, stood next to their father, softly crying into a white handkerchief. Her parents were on her left, silently offering comfort by their presence.

Julia turned from them, choosing to stare at the two dark boxes in the earth. Dignity and civility forced her to remain motionless. If she relaxed her muscles in the slightest, she'd dive right in beside her husband and son, and join them in their resting place.

The priest made the sign of the cross and his voice strained against the loud wind, his umbrella struggling to take flight. It was over. The mourners, comprised of family and friends, began a slow, careful walk across the muddy grounds of the cemetery to their cars. They would drive the short distance to the Bailey family home. Words like 'tragedy' and 'horrible' were plucked by the wind, floating and dancing their way back to her until the endless recital of adjectives made her want to cover her ears. They were the words that had followed her around the last three days. They were all weak words. Useless words. Hopeless words.

Her father took her arm. "Julia, let's go to the car. It's too cold to stay out here, sweetheart."

She stared straight ahead. "Thank you, but no. You can leave. I'm not ready."

There was a pause. Then a deluge of whispers.

"It's all right, I'll stay with her." The deep voice, raspy and hoarse with pain belonged to Chase Donovan, Michael's best friend. He was still holding the umbrella over her, and she knew no one would argue with him. Chase was as rugged and tough as Big Sky country.

She turned slightly, silent as she watched the family walk away. Only when they began opening car doors, far in the distance, did she walk forward.

Chase's presence faded, even though the umbrella above her was a constant. Julia squeezed her eyes shut as she stood next to the open graves. She tried to suck in air. Instead, all the self-control she'd exuded during the funeral hissed out of her mouth and she collapsed like a deflating balloon, lifeless on the cold earth. The pain in her chest that had permanently entrenched itself inside her soul three days ago amplified until it erupted from her mouth in a heaving sob.

"Good-bye, my sweethearts," she whispered, succumbing to the bitter knowledge that all her tomorrows would be without Michael or Matthew.

Rain battered the earth but not her body as the umbrella remained, hovering over her head like a dark halo. She rocked back and forth, her arms clutching her stomach, and prayer poured from her mouth. Prayer to be taken with them.

Her body leaned forward and she heaved, moaning like an old ship before it surrendered to the storm, before it broke under the pressure. But strong arms encircled her, saving her, lifting her up and away from the open earth and she wept with the knowledge that she would see tomorrow.

Chapter One

Five years later

Julia took a deep breath, shutting off her ignition and headlights as she stared at the red-brick Georgian home. Her mother-in-law had loved the Georgian architecture that she had grown up with from her childhood back east, and they'd had the home custom built years ago. Even though it wasn't typical in their rural area of Montana, the home was lovely. It hadn't changed at all. Stately, with black shutters and double-hung windows, and a matching black door, the house beckoned. A large, round boxwood wreath with a red ribbon adorned the front door. The front hall light glowed through the arched transom window, and Julia could still picture the delicate crystal chandelier inside. Towering ponderosa pines flanked the driveway, the tips of the branches almost forming an arch. Snow lined each limb, as though they had been meticulously painted on, one by one.

Five years. It had been five years since she had visited her in-laws. She owed them a visit much earlier. She closed her eyes and leaned her head back. She should have come when her father-in-law had been diagnosed with prostate cancer, but she hadn't. By that time she'd uncovered the disturbing truth about Michael and she couldn't deal with coming back here and facing all of them. But Shadow Creek had also been her home, and these people were her family.

She opened her eyes again and gave a little nod. Well, she was here now for Christmas. She wrapped her hands around the leather handle of her small tote and clutched her purse. The crisp, cold winter air greeted her as she stepped outside her car, cooling her flushed face. It smelled the same—fresh, pure. There was nowhere in the world that smelled like Montana. The driveway and walkway had been shoveled and salted, and her boots crunched against the large granules.

Warmth spread through her body as the front door opened even before she'd made it to the front porch. She clamped down hard on her back teeth in an attempt to rein in the tears as Cassandra and Edward appeared.

"My dear, you are here!" Cassandra Bailey called out, the break in her voice audible.

She dashed up the walkway and steps, outrunning the memories of all the times she'd been here with Michael and Matthew. She ran into the arms of the people that had treated her like their own from day one.

Comfort, the kind that could only be offered from a mother, enveloped her. She held on, squeezing Cassandra, restoring the bond they'd had between them. Edward folded her into his arms, and he kissed the top of her head gently before releasing her.

She had come home.

Edward Bailey gently ushered her through the doorway. "Come in, come in."

Julia noticed the lines around their eyes had deepened, and creases that weren't there years ago had claimed their residence. Edward was still tall with a slightly rounded stomach and maintained his aura of dignity. Cassandra, always thin, had now put on weight, making her seem even more maternal.

They each held on to one of her hands and she looked around the entryway. The deep sage colored walls with the crisp white wainscoting were exactly as she remembered; the grand staircase with its dark wood banister had been dressed for the season with fresh cedar roping and luxurious velvet ribbons.

"Cassy, you still have the nicest Christmas decorations I've ever seen," Julia said, squeezing her hand.

"Julia, is that you?" Her sister-in-law Gwen walked down the corridor, drying her hands on a dishtowel. A brown, medium-sized dog bounded past her and up to Julia. Julia laughed as she looked down into the eager face.

Gwen nudged the dog aside gently by her pink collar. "This is Lola. Don't even ask about that name," she said with a frown before wrapping Julia up in a big hug.

Lola nudged Julia a few times until they broke off the hug and she patted the dog's fluffy head. "You are so cute, Lola." The dog, as if agreeing, tilted her head to the side before giving her hand a lick. "I had no idea you had a dog now."

Edward chuckled. "She's Gwen's. We didn't want a dog but she twisted our arm."

Gwen frowned at him. "I read about dogs and how beneficial they are especially when people are sick."

"Well, there are no sick people around here," Edward said with a shake of his gray head. "Now enough of this standing in the hallway like some stranger. Come in the kitchen. You ladies can do all that hugging once we've had a piece of that pie." He ushered them all down the hallway. Lola trotted dutifully along behind him.

Gwen whispered to Julia as they walked, "He says she's

my dog, but those two became the best of friends. She even went to each treatment Dad had at the hospital."

"She watched over him every day when we'd come back too." Cassy inhaled sharply and plunked her hands on her wide hips as they stood in the doorway of the kitchen. Edward had a knife in his hand and was ready to slice into the pie on the kitchen counter.

"Edward Bailey, put down the knife."

Edward sighed and did exactly as his wife told him, though a few grumbles did escape his mouth.

Julia laughed. "I'm glad to see your appreciation for pie hasn't changed."

"It's gotten worse," Cassy said, marching over and snatching up the knife. "Dr. Hart says he needs to watch how many sweets he eats."

"Well, it's the holiday season and it's not every day a man's favorite daughter-in-law comes home," he said with a wink. His weathered face crinkled slightly as he chuckled and settled himself at the head of the table. Lola rested at his feet. Edward patted the place setting beside him and waved Julia over.

"I can see how it would be hard to resist. It smells so good in here," Julia said, settling in beside him. The long, black farmhouse table was set with quilted, holly and berry placemats and a bright red poinsettia sat in the middle. The country kitchen was toasty, the granite counters filled with canisters of flour and sugar and mixing bowls. They had all changed, but this house was exactly the same.

"I just pulled apple pie and cranberry muffins out of the oven," Gwen said, flashing a smile as she arranged the muffins on a red Santa plate.

Cassandra poured coffee into matching Santa mugs and walked them over to the table.

"Can I help?" Julia asked, rising. Five years ago she would

have been busy keeping Matthew away from the sweets until they were ready. She could think about that now without crying, if she didn't think about it too long.

"Not at all. You've had a long drive, and we want you to sit and relax. You're home, my dear, back in Shadow Creek," Cassandra said, pausing in the middle of the kitchen. Her faded blue eyes shone with emotion and Julia swallowed past the lump in her throat as she smiled at her mother-in-law.

"We've missed you," Edward said, leaning forward and patting her hand. She placed hers atop his, cherishing the warmth from his large, leathery hand. "Cassy couldn't sleep all night. Kept tossing and turning, she was so excited."

Cassandra handed them their mugs of coffee. "Oh I wasn't the only one! How many times did you ask what time she was supposed to arrive today?"

Edward chuckled and Julia basked in their company. She was ready for this now.

"You have all been on my mind and there hasn't been a day where I haven't thought of you. Edward, I owe you an apology for not being here this past year."

"Nonsense. We all did what we had to. We mourn in our own way and none of us begrudge you that. We're happy you're here now. I'm fine. I'm a tough old goat. It's going to take a hell of a lot more than cancer to kick my old butt."

Julia smiled at him. "I'm glad to hear that."

"And how are your parents doing, dear?"

"They're doing really well. Off to visit my mom's sister on the East Coast. They haven't been out there, since…since I went back to live in the city. But when I told them I was coming here this year, I twisted their arms to go." The last few years her parents had been by her side constantly. Julia insisted that this year they get their lives back and do all the things they'd put on hold for five years. She knew they'd agree when they heard she was going back to Shadow Creek.

Cassandra smiled, sitting down. "Oh, that's good. I'm glad your mom is going to see her sister. It looks like we might have another Christmas visitor."

"Who?"

Cassandra smiled. "Jack."

Julia gasped and tears filled her eyes automatically. Jack. Michael's twin brother. She hadn't been the only one who'd run from Shadow Creek after the accident. Jack had taken off, without warning, leaving only a note saying good-bye. He called and he wrote, but he hadn't been home since.

Edward stared out the French doors into the back yard. White twinkling lights were wrapped around the deck railing. "About time that boy came home."

Gwen groaned, sitting down at the table across from her. "I didn't say he was coming home for sure. All I said was that I tried."

Edward reached down to pat Lola's head. "He will. I feel it."

Julia watched as he took a sip of his coffee. Jack and Michael had been connected in a way that none of them could truly understand. They were different and the same. Twins. Best friends. Michael's death had ripped him apart. As it had all of them. She would never tell them about Michael. It would only add new wounds.

Cassandra smiled, Julia giving her smile extra vivacity. "We can only pray, Julia. Now, why don't we dig into some of this delicious pie and then you can get all settled in the guest room, dear."

"Thanks, Cassandra," she whispered, taking a long sip of the velvety coffee. She wrapped her hands around the mug and settled into the black ladder-back chair, trying to look at ease.

"Tell me what you think of that pie. No holding back, I can take it," Gwen said, leaning forward.

Julia sliced through the flaky crust with her fork and lifted the pie to her lips. "You always were the best baker." She closed her eyes for a moment and was greeted with a jolt of warm apples and cinnamon. "Omigod, good."

Gwen tucked a shiny strand of brown hair behind her ear and then smiled, leaning forward. "Lily and I are finally ready to open our chocolate shop."

Julia sucked in a breath. "Oh, I'm so happy for you!"

"We're very proud of Gwen. She's been saving and working like crazy to make this a reality," Edward said, winking at his daughter. "Lily too. The two of them deserve it."

Julia clutched the mug of coffee closer to her as she thought of Lily. When Jack had skipped town, it wasn't just his family he'd abandoned. Lily had been his fiancée, the woman they all knew he would one day marry. "How's Lily doing?"

Gwen frowned, stabbing her piece of pie a little too forcefully, apples oozing out of the sides. "She's okay. *Now*. But it took her a while. And if my big brother does come home this Christmas, he'll have a hell of a lot of apologizing to do."

"I don't want to hear any of that," Cassy whispered, clutching her hands to the side of the table and leaning forward. "If my boy comes home this Christmas, we are all going to welcome him, hug him and—"

"I know, Mom. I want him home too. I can still be hurt for him leaving us and for ditching Lily. But, of course I want Jack home," Gwen said, resting her fork on the table, the pie never reaching her lips.

"Hello," a deep voice, an unmistakeable voice, boomed from the entrance and barrelled into her memories. The voice was followed by fast little footsteps. Lola stood and ran toward the guests. Julia looked first at the little girl she had only seen in pictures for the last five years. Then she looked up at the man that had remained in her thoughts every day since she left Shadow Creek.

Chase Donovan filled the kitchen doorway and every square inch of her mind.

A familiar, comforting, hot-chocolatey warmth billowed over her as his gaze landed on her. Waves of memories lapped in, one by one until her mind was flooded with Chase. He had saved her, repeatedly in the month following Michael and Matthew's death. Chase, with his inky black hair and midnight blue eyes was even more handsome than when she'd first met him. All soft lines were replaced with beautiful angles and hollows. His features were clearly defined; the planes of his strong jaw contrasting with a surprisingly sensual mouth. It was almost unexpected, the only soft spot on his otherwise masculine face. The long, thin scar below his ear and down his jaw was the only flaw on an otherwise impossibly beautiful face. He was tall, and built like a man who knew how to fight. But Chase had only ever shown her tenderness. He'd always been a man who had the ability to make women's pulses beat faster and their hearts swell with hope.

"Good to see you, Julia," he said gruffly.

She stood, wondering why now it felt so awkward. She had cried on his shoulder what must have been hundreds of times. He'd held her in his arms. He'd carried her away from her darkest thoughts on her darkest days. And yet now, five years later, she hesitated a few seconds before rounding the table and then into his arms. He folded her up against his hard chest, and the weight of his arms around her sheltered her like no one else could.

"I'm so damn happy you came home for Christmas," he whispered against her hair, and the raw emotion in his deep voice rapped quietly against all the closed doors inside her soul.

There was a tug on her sweater. "Auntie Julia, it's me,

Maggie!"

Julia stepped away from Chase and looked down at the little girl who looked very much like her daddy. She knelt down to give the little girl a big hug, her heart swelling as Maggie's small arms wrapped around her neck. Julia pulled back to look at her.

"You have grown so much! You're so much bigger than last year's Christmas card!"

Maggie nodded rapidly. "It's true, I'm growing up! I'm going to be as tall as Daddy."

Chase chuckled, ruffling the top of her shiny head with his hand.

"I'm in grade two now," Maggie continued, her eyes glued to Julia's. Matthew would have been in grade two as well. Chase's wife had gotten pregnant with Maggie a few months after Julia. Julia smiled at the little girl, silencing the voices of her memories. She had prepared herself for seeing Maggie again. It had taken a long time to be able to look at a child without wanting to curl back inside herself. But Maggie was different. Julia sensed everyone watching her, worried that seeing Maggie would sadden her.

She straightened up and smiled down at her. "And how's grade two going?"

"Tough. There's homework and stuff."

"Maggie, I saved you a piece of pie," Gwen called, placing a plate of pie and a glass of milk on the kitchen table. Maggie skipped over to the chair beside Gwen and sat down. "Thanks, Auntie Gwen."

"She inherited my sweet tooth," Chase said, shooting her a lopsided grin as they settled back into their chairs.

Cassandra passed Chase a plate filled with pie and a cup of coffee. "Thanks, Cassy, this is just what I needed."

She patted his shoulder before sitting down.

"You better eat all that pie, Julia," Cassandra said, wagging her fork at her. "You've gotten far too thin."

She felt Chase's eyes on her and she looked down at her plate. The weird, fluttery feeling in her stomach had nothing to do with wanting more pie. "I eat, I eat," she said, picking up her fork. Of course she ate. But eating for one was different. Not having anyone to cook for, bake for, fuss for, took the joy out of eating. She hated cooking for herself.

"Julia looks great. I wish I had that problem," Gwen said with a laugh. Julia caught the hint of embarrassment in her voice as she spoke. She had noticed that her sister-in-law had put on weight since she'd last seen her. But Gwen was as pretty as ever and she wouldn't have guessed it was an issue. She had the same coloring as her brothers—brown hair with streaks of blond and hazelnut colored eyes. All three Bailey children were stunning, extra pounds or not.

"You're as gorgeous as always, Gwen," Chase said.

Gwen rolled her eyes and gave him a light punch on the side of his arm. "And *you* are as charming as always."

"Guess what, everyone?" Maggie was sitting on her knees looking around the table and she clanked her fork against her glass.

Chase reached over with a groan, holding on to the glass as it tipped precariously to one side. "All right, Maggie, I think you have everyone's attention now," he said, his deep voice laced with laughter.

Maggie nodded. "Since I'm in grade two this year, I get to have a real serious part in the Shadow Creek School Christmas pageant! I get to be an angel!" she yelled out, almost toppling out of her chair. Edward leaned over to steady her, chuckling.

Everyone offered their congratulations as Maggie efficiently lapped up the pie and the attention with obvious delight.

Chase smiled, whispering under his breath, "I already heard the news on the drive over here, five times, complete with arm gestures and a rousing rendition of 'O Holy Night.'"

Julia swallowed her laugh. "When is the pageant?"

"December first," Chase said.

"You're coming too, right, Auntie Julia?" Maggie asked, stuffing a forkful of pie in her mouth. A glob of apples slid down her face and onto the table.

Julia smiled at the little girl and leaned forward, wiping her face with a Santa napkin. "I'd love to, Maggie."

"We're all going. The night of the pageant is the highlight of the season at the stage in the park, followed by the candle and tree lighting in the town square," Cassandra said. The candle lighting ceremony had been a Shadow Creek tradition dating back to the founding of the town. Each year, in December, people would gather in front of the old courthouse dressed warmly for the winter night. A candle would be lit by the mayor and then slowly, one by one, the flame would get passed until everyone had a lit candle. Choirs would stand on street corners, townspeople would stroll and shopkeepers would keep their doors open until midnight. Julia hadn't been in six years but the ceremony held some of her dearest Christmas memories.

"And my dad is the sheriff so he has to go all dressed up in his uniform and everything," Maggie said. "He's really important around here. Catches bad guys and stuff."

Chase was shaking his head. "Well, in a town like Shadow Creek, Maggie, there's not many bad guys."

"Not just this town, the entire surrounding area. Don't go being modest on us, son. You're the youngest sheriff in history for this area."

Chase shrugged, almost looking uncomfortable with the praise. "Thanks, Edward. You can see I come here because of my fan club," he said, a small smile tugging at one corner of his mouth. "And the food. Definitely the food," he added, giving Julia a wink.

Julia smiled, the warmth from his stare a soothing balm on her conflicted feelings. "I came for the food too," Julia said. It was good to laugh with these people again.

"Good. I don't care what it was that brought you back, my dear. But we're happy to have you home," Cassandra said. The tears in her eyes drowned the laughter at the table.

Julia placed her fork down gently. "I'm here because of all of you. I've missed you so much," she whispered, wanting to say more, but knowing that if she did, she would cry. But it was as though everyone knew because no one said anything.

"Don't worry, Auntie Julia. We're all here so you don't need to miss us anymore," Maggie said with a big grin. "And Daddy said he's really happy you're home. He even said it to the pretty picture of you hanging on our fridge. It's right beside the Luigi's Pizza delivery magnet so first I thought he was ordering pizza."

"Maggie."

Julia choked on her coffee while Chase attempted to reel in his daughter's dialogue. A rush of heat flooded her insides. It shouldn't have. The comment was innocent. Chase would never think of her in that way. But the blue eyes that connected with hers for a moment flickered with…something.

"That's right. Happy you're back. Love Luigi, he's saved us many times." He stood abruptly, his chair scraping against the floor. "We need to get going though, just wanted to stop in and say hi. Tomorrow is a school day, Maggie."

Maggie nodded. "I have a spelling test tomorrow," she said, jumping off her chair. Her dark hair bounced around her as she hopped out of the kitchen. Everyone stood and followed them to the door. Spelling tests and Christmas pageants. It all sounded so wonderful, so warm. Emotion constricted her throat as Chase crouched down and helped his daughter into her pink puffer coat and adjusted her *Hello Kitty* hat on her head. Then he stood and pulled on a black leather jacket and gloves.

Everyone said their good-byes and Julia stood there, watching as he and Maggie made their way down the front walkway. Cassy, Edward, and Gwen walked back to the kitchen chattering about the candle lighting ceremony. She looked down at Lola, who sat quietly by her side. Julia placed her hand on the doorknob, for a second feeling a connection to the man that had been holding it moments before. She watched as Chase made sure Maggie was buckled in and then shut her door. He rounded the front of his SUV and paused. She squeezed the doorknob, her palms turning sweaty as he made eye contact with her.

Chase stood there, stoic and tall, motionless as flakes of white snow drifted around him. He raised his hand a second later and gave her a wave before climbing in behind the wheel. She forced a smile on her face and awkwardly raised her hand. The image of him that day at the funeral tiptoed into her mind and dashed through her body, finding refuge somewhere in her heart.

Chapter Two

"Hey, Sheriff!"

Chase muttered a curse under his breath and turned to look at the young officer jogging over to him. "Meyers, unless you're about to tell me that the Grinch is robbing the bank, hit the road. Today is the first afternoon I've had off in three months. I've got no intention of getting lured back to work."

"Uh, no, no, of course not," the young man stuttered, almost tripping over his feet as well as his words. Chase leaned back against his Expedition and crossed his arms. He tried to look extra intimidating, in an effort to speed along the verbal rambling.

Downtown Shadow Creek was about as bustling as a little town could get at Christmas. It had all the things that tourists loved—cedar strung over shop windows, wreaths hung from each black coach lamp on the main street, and shopkeepers that outdid themselves with store displays. Even he had to admit, if he was into the whole Norman Rockwell scene, and he was not, it was pretty nice, and his daughter got a kick out of it. Seeing her face, hearing her laughter, made all of it worth it.

"So then what can I do for you?" Chase asked after a few seconds of Officer Meyers standing still, staring at him like he was going to ask him out on a date.

"I need to ask you something." Chase frowned as Meyers kicked some snow around with his boot, and didn't continue.

"Meyers, out with it. I gotta pick up my daughter in five minutes."

"Right. Right. Um, so, the thing is, Mayor Mayberry came by the station and asked if you'd be willing to dress up as Santa Claus on the night of the candle lighting."

Chase stared at the top of his head, his words not sinking in right away. "Excuse me?"

"You know, Santa. The man who dresses up in a red suit."

"I know who Santa is." The only problem with small towns, he'd discovered, was the sense of amity everyone had. So much so apparently that the mayor actually thought he would dress up as Santa Claus. He loved his job, but not that much.

Going into law enforcement had been a no-brainer for him. To serve and protect. That's what he'd always done as a kid, as an adult. The town was small, the regional area rural and comprised of mostly decent people. There were aspects, certain people and types of crimes that made his gut twist and kept him up some nights, but that was all part of the job. "So why didn't Mayberry ask me himself?"

"I think he might have been scared to, Sheriff."

Chase scowled. "Why the hell are you here asking me?"

"He didn't think you'd go for the idea and all the guys nominated me to come and ask you."

Of course they did. Ask the rookie to come out and do their dirty work. That and probably the fact that Mayberry was Meyers's uncle. If you weren't related to someone in Shadow Creek, then your neighbor definitely was. Or your parents grew up together. He sighed as the young constable looked at him with a rather hopeful stare. Obviously, Meyers didn't know him well enough. *Santa, my ass.* "I'm the sheriff, not a freaking sideshow. The answer is no. I'll talk to your uncle." Chase added that last part when it looked like the young officer was about to cry at the thought of having to speak with the mayor. He understood. Mayor Mayberry was a walking-talking Roly Poly doll. And once the man started talking, the verbal diarrhea continued indefinitely. The only one who talked more than the mayor was his wife, Marlene Mayberry.

Meyers smiled with relief and backed up a step. "Thanks, Sheriff."

Across the street, a familiar brunette in a red coat entered his line of vision, slowing outside the Christmas tree lot. His gut clenched, a familiar feeling whenever Julia was around. "Go back to work, Meyers," Chase said, jogging across the street without waiting for a reply.

When he'd seen Julia last night, the first time in five years, the love he'd had for her hit him in the gut. And then, as he'd done in the past, he'd swallowed it down.

He'd come to the conclusion before she came home for Christmas that he needed to stop feeling guilty about his feelings for her. He'd never done anything to let on that he was in love with Julia. Never to Michael, Jack, or Julia. It had been his secret and he'd been willing to go on his whole life without ever letting it out.

More than anything, more than his feelings for her, his wanting her, he wanted a happy ending for her. He wanted their little boy to be alive. He wanted Michael to be alive.

Nothing had ever come close to hurting more than when he found out about the accident. And then witnessing the pure hell Julia went through. He vowed to his friend the day of the funeral that he would watch out for her. But then she was packing up and tearfully trying to tell him why she couldn't stay in Shadow Creek, and hell, he couldn't blame her one bit.

But now she was back. And God, he'd missed her.

"Looking for a Christmas tree?"

She shot him a surprised glance, looking over at him. "Oh, hey, Chase." Her full lips pulled into a gorgeous smile and he cursed himself. He didn't need to be noticing her mouth. He turned away to look at the lot full of trees.

"No, I just love the smell. I was out for a walk and thought I might do some Christmas shopping."

"You walked here?"

She nodded. The tip of her nose was pink and her cheeks were rosy. "I had to. They have all been force-feeding me pies and cookies. This morning, I walked into the kitchen to find Edward sitting alone at the kitchen table eating pie. Minutes later Cassy comes in and he shoved the pie at me, and I had to pretend it was mine and eat it! I'm not going to fit into my clothes by Christmas."

Chase laughed and tried not to sound like he was choking. He didn't want to think of her figure. Julia thought it was some nonchalant ha-ha comment, while he thought of beautiful curves. Perfect curves. "I don't think you have anything to worry about." He wanted to add that he thought all her pounds were in the nicest places, but he had no intention of coming off like some sort of creep. Or someone who'd been in love with her since high school. Or like someone who hung her picture on the front of his refrigerator door next to Luigi the pizza guy. Dammit.

"I was thinking of dropping into Jack and Jill's to pick up some gifts for Maggie."

He shook his head. "Don't worry about—"

"Are you kidding me? I love that old toy shop and I love that little girl of yours. It's still there, isn't it?" she asked, turning around to look in the direction of the town's only toy store.

He clenched his teeth hard. He didn't want Julia going into a toy store buying gifts for his daughter when she should have been going in there to buy gifts for her son. She had never stopped communicating with them, even the first Christmas after she left she always sent a card and a gift for Maggie. He followed her gaze and they stared at the little yellow building. The large window showcased a vintage model locomotive and even from across the road he could make out the elaborate toy village surrounding the moving train. "Yeah, that place is practically a landmark. Mrs. Bowman retired last year, but her daughter, Sabrina, took it over."

Julia was smiling when she turned back to look at him. "Great, I haven't seen Sabrina in years, I'll be sure to stop by. Hey, aren't you working today?"

He shook his head. "No, my afternoon off. I'm just waiting to pick up Maggie."

She tucked her hands into her coat. "Oh that's nice. She's so sweet, Chase. I mean, you've done a great job raising her."

He smiled back, thinking of his daughter. Maggie was the best thing in his life. She had drawn out all the good in him, forced it out of him until he became the father he was meant to be. And he owed it to her. He'd failed her once, by picking the wrong woman. He would never make that mistake again. "Thanks. She's a pretty incredible kid, despite her father." He laughed.

Julia looked down, her smile faltering. "I owe you an apology."

He frowned. "For what?"

She looked up at him. "You were there for me and I wasn't around when Sandy left."

Wind whipped her red scarf around her neck and her dark glossy hair swayed just enough that it almost begged him to touch it. He stared into her eyes, into the most genuine eyes he'd ever seen. He shook his head.

"No. No you don't owe me an apology. We were fine. We made it through. Edward, Cassy, and Gwen helped us more than I ever expected. They helped give Maggie the stability and the security she needed. They took on childcare and told me they would be the family I needed. Don't you dare feel bad for leaving. I get it, Julia. You needed to survive and you did what you had to." He owed the Baileys so much. They were the family he'd never had. They were the grandparents he could never give his daughter. He took a step closer to her, taking in the perfect skin, the tip of her nose pink with the cold.

"Thanks."

Chase stood there, wanting to say more, but everything felt so awkward. He wanted to cut through the bull until all that was left was the way they were. He stuffed his hands into the pockets of his leather jacket. "I want to ask you for a favor."

She nodded. "Of course, anything."

"I want to move. I want to list our house and find something else," he said, motioning to the school. "Do you mind if we walk over to stand by the school while we talk?"

"Sure, of course," she said, falling into step beside him. He had an insane need to reach out and grab her hand, and if he were sappy, he'd love to think that this was their everyday reality. Walking to school to pick up their little girl and Maggie would run out, the smile on her face and the security in her eyes that of a child who'd never known the pain of having a parent walk out on them. Crap. Two days back in town and the woman he'd dreamed about since he was a teenager was now making him crave all those naive dreams he'd had when he was a boy, when he'd vowed to himself to do better than his parents had done by him. Thanks to Sandy, he'd failed Maggie, and all his dreams had turned to hell.

"I didn't know you were thinking of moving."

He glanced over at her as they stood a bit further away from the group of waiting parents. "I mean, I don't want you to have to work over Christmas or anything. It's not a rush. I know you've got your agency back in the city, I just thought —"

"Hey, I'd love to," she said, her hand on his arm. His muscles flexed at the friendly touch, causing an avalanche of unwanted feelings. "I didn't realize you were thinking of selling the place."

He scraped his fingers through his hair. "Yeah. I think it's time to close that door on Sandy, you know? I feel like I need a new place. A fresh start. It's been long enough."

"Does she ever call?"

"Nothing. I stopped waiting for her to come back after a year."

"God, I'm so sorry."

He shrugged. He didn't want to talk about Sandy. He didn't want to be standing out here in a crowd. He wanted to be alone with Julia. He wanted to hear everything about the last five years. Her job, her life back in the city, and if he were brutally honest with himself, he wanted to know if there was a man in her life.

He glanced over at her and she was still staring at him with those green eyes of hers. "It's okay. I'm over it. And I've done my best to make sure Maggie is over it, though sometimes I think I'm deluding myself. A kid will never get over a parent walking out." He knew that from personal experience. That hole, that bullet wound that could never properly heal, because the bullet remained inside. That's what it was like.

"Maggie is happy and well-adjusted, it's so obvious."

He nodded. "I hope so. I did my best. That's part of the reason I want to find a new place. I want her to have a home that's only filled with happiness." He tossed aside the memories of that first year. He'd been a wreck. She'd been a wreck. But they'd managed. He learned how to be a single dad, and the two of them were their own little family. And the way his little girl looked at him made him feel like he'd done okay. It had taken two years to win back the trust that Sandy had robbed Maggie of, and if he ever saw her again…

"Well, it's easy for me to pull up a bunch of listings."

"I know the place I want."

"Really?"

He nodded. "On Tall Pines Street, there's a log house that looks like it needs some work. But it has a view of the mountains. It's got a huge backyard for Maggie. Four bedrooms. Big old front porch. It's out of town but a short drive in for me. It's vacant and it has been for almost a year."

"It sounds perfect, Chase. How about I look it up and call the listing agent to make an appointment?"

"I bet you can already guess who the listing agent is," he said with a groan.

She smiled. "Marlene Mayberry?"

"The one and only."

"This should be fun," she said with a laugh. "It seems she still has the real estate market cornered in Shadow Creek."

"The Mayberrys still own half the town. No sign of retiring yet. Maybe if they can convince one of their kids to move back to town, they could pass off some of their assets and step down."

"I don't think any of their kids could stand living under their dictatorship," Julia said under her breath.

He nodded. "You're probably right."

"I'll talk to Marlene and set something up. What's your schedule like?"

He grunted. "Non-stop, but you get me a time and I'll make it happen. Can you try and get something soon? I was thinking since it's vacant, maybe I could surprise Maggie with it for Christmas."

Her mouth opened. "By Christmas? That's so much work. You have to pack and—"

"I'll hire a company."

She nodded. "Of course. I think that's so sweet of you, it will make for an unforgettable Christmas, and you both deserve it," she said, her voice lowering to a whisper. "Okay, I'll give them a call and be careful not to let on that we really want it and hopefully we can get in to see it tomorrow."

We really want it. He knew she didn't mean anything by it, but for a second he let himself imagine what it would be like to be there as a family, all three of them. He shrugged that thought off. He needed to get a hold of himself. And as for deserving an unforgettable Christmas, well hell, no one deserved it more than Julia. "You're sure you don't mind working while you're here?"

"This isn't work, trust me. This is fun. It'll give me something to do. And I'm showing Gwen and Lily a retail space tomorrow too—and of course when I called the office to book the appointment, I found out that Marlene has that listing as well. Looks like I'll be overdosing on the Mayberrys soon, thanks to all of you."

He barked out a laugh. "Sorry about that, though I gotta say, I'm really happy for Gwen and Lily, glad they're finally going through with it."

"I know, me too. All we need is Jack to come home."

He nodded. He missed his friend. He heard from Jack every now and then, a quick email, nothing more. Only Chase and Gwen had been around after Michael and Matthew died, the only ones there to offer Edward and Cassy support. But he didn't resent Jack, and he knew his friend was going to have to face hell when he finally came back to town, especially when he saw Lily again.

Julia turned to a group of women, her gaze narrowing as she looked back up at him. "Is that your personal fan club over there, Sheriff?" Her lips had turned up into a mischievous little smile and he searched her eyes for even a spark of jealousy. Of course it wasn't there and how pathetic was he for wishing? He glanced over at the three women who made a habit of being around wherever he was.

He shrugged. "No fan club."

"Chase, I remember exactly what you were like before Sandy," she said, lifting her brows and pursing her lips. How freaking happy was he that she was teasing him? Back when they all hung out together, one of his favorite things about Julia was her ability to tease. She had a sharp wit and she observed things like no one else he knew.

He crossed his arms over his chest, smiled down at her, and then took a step closer because he couldn't stand back. Chase had waited forever for this woman, and now she was back, even if it was only for the holidays. He heard her breath catch slightly and her green eyes lit in a way that told him she was very aware of him as well—and hell if that didn't make him as happy as a teenager asking a girl out on a first date. "Really? And what exactly was I like?"

She crossed her arms and narrowed her eyes, an adorable smirk on her face. "You had your blondes-only club as I recall."

He choked down his laugh. Yeah. That had been after he discovered all brunettes reminded him of Julia. And he hadn't wanted to go to bed with a woman while he was thinking of his best friend's wife. So he'd stuck to blondes. No way in hell would he ever tell Julia that. "Well, I was young and cocky."

She nudged her chin in the direction of the women. "So it's merely a coincidence that those women are all blondes?"

He nodded and rolled back on his heels. "What can I say, that's who I attract I guess. It's the cross I bear."

Her squeal of laughter made him smile, as did the way she leaned a little closer to him.

He fisted his hands and shoved them into his pockets, because he didn't trust himself to not pull her in close. "And the whole cop thing seems to appeal for some reason."

She gave him a sidelong glance, turning away just as he caught a glimpse of something in her eyes. "I couldn't imagine why. So they're part of the Sheriff Donovan fan club?"

"No fan club."

She looked down for a moment. "Chase, you always had a fan club."

"I'm not into the whole dating scene." Her head snapped up and he held her gaze. He wanted her to know that. He wasn't a guy who was carefree anymore. He didn't consider himself single, not with a daughter, and hell, there was no one he wanted more than Julia.

She didn't say anything for a long moment. "Really?"

He gave her a quick nod. "The last thing I want is for Maggie to be confused. I don't want her seeing me with a woman that won't be around forever."

Several moments went by and they just stood there. Her hand was close to his and he wanted nothing more than to tug her close to him and finally hold her and kiss the woman he'd wanted for so many years. There had always been something or someone in the way. Even now, there was the memory of his best friend, the man she'd loved more than anything. How the hell could he compete with the memory of the perfect man?

The front doors of the red brick school burst open and kids ran out, scattering across the yard, interrupting his thoughts. He waved as he spotted the bright pink pom-pom on the top of Maggie's hat. His daughter's eyes connected with his and that feeling he always got when she smiled at him, filled his chest. She was running over to them, and he knew she was excited that Julia was there too.

"Daddy!" she yelled and he picked her in a big hug, but

seconds later she was squirming out of his arms to say hi to Julia.

"I'm so happy you're here," she said to Julia who reached out to hug her.

"I'm so happy to see you too, sweetie." Julia backed up a step, folding her arms across her chest and even before he looked into her eyes he sensed the distance she put between them. "I should let you two get on with your afternoon off."

"Come with us! Daddy said we're going tobogganing."

Julia glanced up at him, and he realized he was actually holding his breath. He may have even been more excited than his daughter. "That sounds like fun, thank you so much for inviting me, Maggie. But I'm going to have to pass this time because I have a few errands to run." She was frowning, the regret etched on the side of her lips.

He squashed his disappointment and held out his hand for Maggie, feeling better as her small hand clutched his. He and Maggie had gotten along fine for years.

"It's okay, Auntie Julia. Don't feel bad, you didn't know. Maybe we'll see each other tomorrow."

"I'm looking forward to it, sweetie." Julia leaned down and gave Maggie a kiss and then looked up at him. "I'll, um, be in touch as soon as I get an appointment time."

He nodded, watching as she walked through the crowd of people by herself.

Julia was the only woman he'd trust with his daughter's heart.

Chapter Three

Julia twisted the key in the old lock and then jiggled it as it refused to budge. Gwen and Lily stood silently beside her. Julia gave the key one final jiggle and then felt the mechanism release. She shot them both a quick smile before pushing the old wooden door open. She stepped inside and held the door open for them. The musky scent of the old building clung to the air and a fine layer of dirt seemed to cover everything.

Gwen stood in the middle of the open space, a stream of dust-filled sunlight highlighting her smile. "Omigod. This is perfect. Beyond perfect."

Julia smiled and looked around. Lily was behind the counter, running her hand along the smooth, white marbled top counter. The women had their eye on the old Apothecary building for a few months now and asked that this be the first stop on their search for a retail venue for their handmade chocolate shop. Antique bronze schoolhouse light fixtures hung from the worn patterned tin ceiling and the wide, wooden plank floors creaked as she walked across to join Lily at the counter.

She placed her listing file on the counter and peeled off her leather gloves. "What do you think, Lily?"

Lily looked up at her, a smile gracing her pretty face. "I think Gwen's right. This place is perfect."

"It is so charming," Julia said, looking through the large, lattice window that faced Main Street. Across the road was the Shadow Creek Book Nook. It had been there for as long as she could remember, the only bookstore in town. Mr. Palmer was in the window, only the top of his gray head visible as he bent over the life-size stuffed Santa who sat in front of a fake brick fireplace reading a book. It was the same display year after year, but no one ever grew tired of it. It was like an heirloom Christmas tree ornament, forgotten throughout the year and then cherished and prized as it made its appearance for the holidays.

Gwen walked over to them and Julia tore her eyes from the comforting image in the window. "Can we see the kitchen?"

Julia nodded, picking up her file. "Definitely." They walked toward the green swinging door with the small circular window opening. "Fingers crossed this is as nice as the rest of the front." She stood back and let the women check out the appliances and workspace. The area was small, but considering their needs it might work.

"I love this place. I get such a good vibe here," Gwen said.

Lily walked to the back door. "Me too." She opened it and there was a small back parking lot and two garbage bins. "It has parking too?"

Julia nodded. "Yup. There's enough room for two vehicles, which is great." They walked around the kitchen, opening cupboard doors and appliances. "So after the apothecary left, it looks like this was converted into a coffee shop, right?"

Gwen nodded. "Yes, but it never really took off. The owners were from out of town and they weren't that pleasant and their baked goods weren't great."

Customer service and approachability were everything in a small town. Shadow Creek was all about personal connections and friendly chit-chat. People shopped locally not only out of convenience but for the social connection.

"All the appliances look great and the work surface is perfect. Even though it's a little rough around the edges, I think we can make this work," Lily said, smoothing her hand across the stainless steel island.

"Yes, according to the listing all the appliances were installed for the previous owners, so they can't be more than a few years old."

"Do you think the rent is negotiable?"

Julia flipped open the file and scanned the listing details. "Well, according to this, it's been listed for almost a year, and judging by the condition of this place, we should be able to negotiate a better price. I can list all the deficiencies, all the repairs you'd have to make and hopefully the owner will either compensate for the repairs or arrange for them to be done."

Lily frowned. "But if he arranges for them to be done, they might not be what we have in mind."

Julia nodded. "True, but I can stipulate that any renovations they make have to be approved by you both."

Gwen leaned against the counter. "Okay. So how much do you think we can take off this rent?"

Julia tilted her head to the side. "How far off are we? You've gotten approved for a start-up loan, right?"

They both nodded. "Yeah, and we are both pooling all the money we've saved," Lily said.

She opened the file on the table, looking over the two pages of listing details and drummed her fingers on the counter. She wanted them to get this place. They both deserved it and she felt she owed Gwen. It was the least she could do for being away for so long. "So do you think you could manage if we had the rent reduced by a third?"

Lily winced. "We were hoping a little more. I guess half would be pushing it?"

Julia blew out a breath. "That's tough, but I'll try my best. We do have a lot going for us, and the likelihood of this place getting rented out in December is minute. It might really appeal to the landlord to have it leased out and off his plate. Of course that does mean I'll be deep in negotiations with Marlene." She bit her lower lip trying to hold back her laugh as the women groaned.

Gwen grimaced slightly, but her eyes sparkled. "So, what do you think, Lily? Should we go for it?"

Lily didn't say anything for a moment and then broke out into a huge smile. "Let's do it!"

The door burst open, a gust of wind and a shock of red infiltrating the small space. "Woo-hoo. Hello, hello!"

Julia smiled across the store as Marlene Mayberry graced them with her flamboyant presence. Her dark hair was sprayed and styled until it glistened unnaturally. Her pale skin was merely a canvas for a vibrant display of red lipstick and rouge, blue eye shadow and thick, black mascara. "Well, I knew when a flurry of calls came in for showings, that it must be our very own Julia Bailey. Oh, you city agents never take a break, do you?"

Julia opened her mouth to reply, but the woman had already swallowed up the steps between them and captured her in a hug, drowning her in the scent of sweet roses.

"So nice to see you, Mrs. Mayberry," she said, trying to pry herself out of the older woman's arms before she choked. Gwen and Lily were practically crying as they attempted to hold in their laughter. Julia quickly looked away from them, knowing their laughter would be contagious.

"It's wonderful to have you back in town, my dear. Just

wonderful. Even if it does mean having some competition," she said with a wink that was slightly delayed as her mascara-filled lashes clumped together.

"Thank you, Mrs. Mayberry. I kept my realtor license in Montana just in case and now that I'm temporarily back here, I'm glad that I did. It's nice to be working with you again. But, it'll just be for the holidays of course. I'll be heading back to Chicago after New Year's." She didn't look at Gwen when she made that statement.

Marlene's face collapsed into a frown. "Oh that is a shame, but I do have some good news for our dear Sheriff Donovan. That house on Tall Pines has his name written all over it. How does ten o'clock tomorrow morning sound for a showing?"

Julia held on to her squeal of delight. "That sounds perfect. I'll confirm with Chase and we'll be there."

"That man is a prize waiting to be claimed," she said with a theatrical sigh. Her large eyes settled on Julia's like an old owl perching onto a branch, scouting for prey.

"Mrs. Mayberry, we are in love with this space," Gwen said, walking over to them and saving Julia. Thank God for her sister-in-law's intervention.

"Excellent, excellent. I'll be waiting for that offer, then, Julia!" She gave her another slow-motion wink. And then as quickly as the woman had entered, did she exit, leaving in her wake only the smell of roses and the faint sense of unease.

The three of them looked at each other, silent for a moment before erupting in a fit of laughter.

Julia stopped after a few moments, squeezing Gwen's hand and looking at both of them. "I promise I will do what it takes to make this place a reality for you two. Whatever you need, okay?"

They both nodded and Gwen leaned forward to give her a hug. "Thanks."

"I didn't know Chase was looking at that house on Tall

Pines."

Julia nodded. The more she thought of her conversation with Chase yesterday, the more she wanted to make this happen for him and Maggie. They deserved a fresh start. The way he'd spoken about Maggie reminded her of the special love she'd had for Matthew. That desire to give him the best, to give him everything she possibly could.

She wanted to help Chase fulfill those dreams for his little girl, and she wanted to spend time with them. That was something she hadn't counted on. Of course she'd been looking forward to seeing them, but she hadn't expected how much, and the connection she felt to Maggie.

"He really deserves the best after all he's been through. He came around constantly after." Gwen paused and looked at the ground for a moment. "After the accident. And he became like another brother to me. Mom and Dad basically adopted him and Maggie. He was their rock, mine too."

Julia blinked away tears as she stared into her sister-in-law's eyes, so much like Michael's. "I feel like crap when I think of how I let you guys down."

Gwen shook her head. "Don't you dare apologize to me. You did what you had to. Let's move beyond this. I just wanted you to know." She cleared her throat and touched Julia's arm. "That Chase is strong. He's a good man."

Julia nodded slowly, sensing more to Gwen's comment. "I know he is." She looked past Gwen to the red-brick school, thinking of yesterday. Maggie and Chase made her yearn for everything she had lost, but even more. If she were honest with herself, she'd admit that what scared her most was not just the yearning for what was gone, but for the possibility of what could be. But that would mean trusting a man again, and that was something she didn't think could ever happen, especially if Chase had known what Michael had done. A part of her didn't want to know.

"He's done so well for himself and Maggie. The bad boy turned cop. Really, I can't think of a better man," Lily said softly, tucking her blonde hair inside her hood. *Ouch* for Jack. No one said anything as Gwen opened the door and they stepped outside, waiting as Julia locked up and placed the key inside the lock box.

"This is turning out to be the best Christmas we've had in years, because of you, Julia." The tears in Gwen's eyes were contagious and she blinked rapidly. Seriously, these people were turning her into a pile of mush.

She walked forward and gave Gwen a hug. "For me too."

"All we need now is for Jack to come home." Gwen pulled away from her and wiped at the fallen tears. "I sent him a long email that has filled him with so much guilt he has no choice but to come home."

Julia smiled. "That would be perfect, but you need to stop with the tears or I'm going to have to start carrying around a box of tissues with me." They laughed, walking away from the shop and to their cars. Jack. She didn't add anything about her own feelings. A part of her wondered how she would react to seeing him. His face. He and Michael had been identical twins, and while she could easily tell them apart she knew there would be no denying his face. Would she see him as a different man? Would she see Michael immediately? Would she be able to look into the identical eyes of the man she lost, that had betrayed her, and know, fully, that they were not the same person?

It took them a moment to realize Lily hadn't fallen into step beside them. They turned around and she was still standing in front of the store. Her dark brown eyes were wide in her pale face and they both walked back to her.

"You think Jack is coming home for Christmas?"

Gwen gasped. "I'm an idiot for blurting that out. I don't know. I told you I had written him, but I still don't know for sure."

Lily shook her head. "No, no. Don't apologize. He's your brother. You've all been through so much and especially with your dad this past year…"

"Still, I love my brother, I always will, but what he did was what I call *jack*-ass behavior."

Lily's face cracked and turned into a smile. They all burst out laughing at Gwen.

"It's a good one, isn't it?" Gwen asked.

"So good," Lily said, swinging her purse over her shoulder. "Jack can come home, and that will be perfect for all of you. It doesn't bother me in the least. I've moved on with Ben. Jack is history," she whispered in a voice that was so heavy with the weight of her hurt that her smile faltered.

Julia knew that weight…

It was the weight of a woman whose heart had been broken by a man.

Chapter Four

Julia sat in the front seat of her rental SUV, parked in the driveway of the house on Tall Pines. She was a few minutes early for the property showing and was catching up on emails while she waited for Chase to arrive. She had taken the entire month off from work, something she hadn't done since she'd started at the real estate office. She wanted to enjoy her time here, and she'd had a feeling that when her vacation was over she'd need a few days to get Shadow Creek out of her mind before returning to work.

She quickly re-read the text from Marlene saying she was making headway with the offer on the chocolate shop. Satisfied with that, she sent a quick text to Gwen and Lily. Then she checked to see if there was any word from Chase. He'd confirmed by text last night that he'd meet her here. He was on call, so he'd mentioned he might be a few minutes late.

She turned up the heat in the car as a gust of wind shook the vehicle slightly and peered out the front dash at the house. She could see why Chase wanted it. It was a traditional log-style ranch house, common in the area, but there was something about the way it was set on the property. The previous owners had obviously gone to great lengths to preserve the towering, old, ponderosa pines and had built the house in what looked like a natural clearing. It was deep-set, far from the road, the mountains as the backdrop. There was a large front porch, and she could practically see Chase standing out there, watching Maggie build a snowman. No, he'd probably be right alongside his little girl, helping. The property was stunning, rugged, and larger-than-life. Much like the man himself.

Chase and Michael and Jack had been best friends. Out of the three of them, Michael had been the different one. He'd followed in his father's footsteps and had become a lawyer. He had been smart, charismatic, a true gentleman. Well, that last part was debateable, considering what she'd found out in the year following his death. Chase and Jack had been the most similar, both of them with an edge, a gruffness that she knew only covered up a heart of gold. Jack…she hadn't seen him since she'd left town. He'd run; just like her, except he not only left his family, he'd walked away from his fiancée.

Chase had stuck around, helped all the Baileys get through the worst days of their lives. He had dragged her out of the hole she'd been living in—enough that she could stand on her own two feet again and start over. But she'd missed him, in a way that surprised her. There had been so many nights she'd yearned for the feel of him, the scent of him, the sound of his voice, the strength of his body. She had gotten used to the silence. She had become stronger than she ever thought possible, but was she ever alone.

She blinked back tears and the sound of tires crunching the gravel and snow-covered long drive pulled her out of her thoughts. A quick glance in the rear-view mirror confirmed the object of her thoughts had arrived. She met Chase outside and was jolted by his smile. His stride was long and powerful, and he turned down the radio on his black vest as he joined her by her car. His hair was windblown and slightly disheveled, but his blue eyes were alert. He was…beautiful. Good grief, this wasn't what she was supposed to be thinking about.

"Hey there, Julia."

She pretended he was just any other client, but that was kind of stupid, because this man knew more about her than anyone else on the planet right now. She forced a normal smile. "Hey, how's your day going?"

"Another day of excitement in Shadow Creek. Was picking up some coffee on my way to the station this morning, and a senior drove his car through the window of the coffee shop, so that's always a fun way to start the day."

Julia gasped and covered her mouth. "What? That's horrible."

He grinned and shrugged. "It happens a lot more than you'd think. He put the car in drive instead of reverse and then, wham," he said, making a sliding motion with his hand.

"Was anyone hurt?"

"No. A bit of bruised male pride for the driver, but that's about it."

She shook her head. She had often wondered how he did what he did. She was also very aware of how he seemed to take everything in stride. Nothing shook Chase.

They walked side by side, and she noticed he blocked a nice portion of the wind. There was about a foot of snow on the ground and she was happy she was wearing her tall boots. "You know, the fact that there's not even one set of footsteps out here tells me maybe there haven't been too many showings on this property."

"Good observation. We've had snow on the ground for two weeks."

"Huh," she said as she deftly punched the code into the lock box. "When I asked Marlene about activity on this place she said it was non-stop." She shot him a look and he gave a short laugh.

"Ready?" she said as the lock released, looking up at him.

He gave her that grin that probably stopped much of the female traffic in Shadow Creek and then nodded. She swung open the wood door but he made her go through it first. They stood in silence in the front entry, looking around. The wooden, wide-plank floors were dusty, but from where they were standing seemed to be in decent shape.

"Not as bad as I was expecting," Chase said, walking further into the house. The electricity was off, but enough light came through the windows that they could easily make out the details. The sound of his boots against the wood floor was the only thing that could be heard other than the occasional rattling of windows from the wind. When they entered the kitchen, Julia gasped.

"Chase, this is beautiful," she said. The kitchen, though dated, had a big island in the center, a U-shaped cooking area that was large, the sink situated over a massive picture window. It was open to a huge family room that boasted high, peaked ceilings with wooden beams and a floor-to-ceiling stone fireplace.

She glanced over at Chase who was leaning against the counter, arms crossed, watching her. She reprimanded herself for noting how good he looked, rugged, masculine lines on display as he stood there. "You like it?"

"Uh, *yeah*? Don't you? Look at the windows, and that view!" The mountains stood majestically in the distance, white-capped and proud. "You don't even need a TV, that view is so beautiful."

"Yeah. I guess Maggie would have a problem with the lack of television, though," he said, one corner of his mouth turned up slightly.

She smiled. "That's true. Don't let her know I even

suggested that. But seriously, look at the beams, the fireplace. I wouldn't change anything."

"What would you do to the kitchen?"

She walked over to it, her heeled boots echoing on the wood floor in the vacant home. She furrowed her brow as she took in the proportions. "I'd do dark cabinets with a slightly distressed finish, you know, masculine. Maybe a large stainless steel built-in refrigerator."

"What about a woman? What would a woman want in here?"

She quickly tore her gaze from his intense one. A woman. Of *course* he was probably dating someone. He should have brought her. Though, that would have been awkward. Well, it shouldn't be awkward, but a part of her didn't want to meet whoever he was with. He did tell her the other day he wasn't into the whole dating scene—for Maggie's sake. But maybe that meant, he wouldn't just date anyone and that he'd actually found the right woman.

She didn't know what to make of the disappointment she felt at the thought of him with someone really special. And what about Maggie? She deserved a nice woman in her life. That little girl had been through so much. Or maybe he wasn't dating anyone at all and was looking into the future to when he would be dating someone...and getting married again. Ugh.

She needed to get her sudden possessive line of thinking toward Chase in line. She cleared her throat and walked to stand in the center of the current U-shape cooking area. "I guess I could see a large, white, farmhouse sink right here, under the window."

He stood there, hands in his pockets, eyes not leaving hers and she had to unbutton her coat, feeling hot. What was wrong with her? Things had never been like this between them. She had never been so aware of his presence, his energy. She turned away from him and gestured with her hands. "I'd place a large, cream colored, distressed island in the middle, the same spot as this one. Maybe with some corbels underneath—nothing too ornate, just to add some custom details, and of course room for seating. That would lighten things up and make it a little more feminine."

He ran his hand over his jaw, not looking impressed. "What's this distressed stuff you're talking about?"

"Oh! It's where the cabinet maker will sand off a little of the paint finish in spots that would normally get wear and tear or make a few subtle dents."

He was silent for a moment. "So I'd be paying for someone to ruin a new piece of wood?"

She laughed. "Sort of, but it looks really great."

He gave her a look that suggested otherwise. Then he flicked his chin in the direction of the great room. "What would you do in there?"

She swung around and made her way into what was so far the most gorgeous room. "Not much, Chase. This room with the fireplace and massive windows is almost perfect. I love the beams. I'd give it a fresh coat of paint—something neutral. A large area rug to anchor the furniture. You don't need window coverings because there's tons of privacy."

"I like more privacy. What would you suggest?"

He was standing beside her now, hands shoved in his pockets. She tried to ignore how good it felt to be here, just the two of them. There was something that felt so right about him, standing beside him, talking to him. She forced her attention back to his question when he looked down at her. "I guess blinds that can give you privacy and then roll up completely so that the view is unobstructed."

"How about furniture?"

She was about to laugh and tease him that she wasn't an interior decorator, but she caught a hint of vulnerability in a face that rarely showed anything but strength. There was also a gleam in his blue depths that made this personal. "Well, you have enough room for a large sectional and maybe a nice square ottoman coffee table," she said, gesturing to the space in front of the fireplace.

He nodded. "Can I buy this online?"

She turned fully to him, crossing her arms. "You online shop?"

He grinned. "I hate shopping. I'd rather shoot myself with my own gun than go shopping. One-clicking appeals to me."

She laughed as they walked toward the bedrooms. "Try Pottery Barn." She stopped abruptly and almost poked him in the chest with her index finger to make a point then stopped short. Somehow it didn't feel like she should touch him, maybe because a part of her wanted to touch him. "Just wait for the sale. Don't buy full price. Seriously."

He gave her a salute and grin that almost made her toes curl. What was wrong with her? Maybe she had missed him even more than she'd realized.

She had met Chase the same day she'd met Michael. Her family had moved to Shadow Creek when she'd started her second to last year of high school. She still remembered exactly what Chase had looked like that day. It was slightly disconcerting that she remembered even more about the way he'd looked, exactly what he was wearing, and the expression on his face. He didn't have a scar back then; that had happened his first year on the force. Chase had always been larger than life to her, slightly intimidating. He'd had an edge to him. Michael had been the safe, responsible choice. It was ironic it was only she and Chase still standing, both having been burned by their partners. But no matter what Michael had done, he'd given her the most beautiful baby boy to love, and for that she would never regret marrying him.

"You all right?" He approached her and she swallowed

repeatedly, her heartbeat accelerating in a way that it shouldn't. It was this house, that was it. It was quiet, intimate and she was here helping him decide on a place for his little family, like she was someone that fit into his day-to-day life. She didn't. Not anymore. He seemed to swallow up the hallway, and for a second she had a flash of being held in his arms and she remembered the warmth, the safety she'd felt against his hard chest. She remembered his clean, crisp scent as she sat in his arms, crying.

"Jules?" he repeated, saying her name in that way that made her wish…things she hadn't in many years. Her days of marriage and kids were over, the scars left behind too deep to ever make her want to risk it all again.

"Yep. Totally fine," she said, shooting him what she hoped was a casual smile and then sidestepped him and stood at the threshold of the master bedroom.

"This is nice," he said, standing beside her, his arm brushing against hers. Even though they both still had their jackets on, she felt the touch sear through her. She kept her eyes trained on the features of the room.

"It's beautiful. Vaulted ceilings again. That's so gorgeous, and I love that the view is the back of the house so you can wake up and see the mountains every day," she said, trying to act like a real estate professional as she crossed the room. She was also trying not to think of him in bed. Waking up, by himself or with someone else…which of course was none of her business.

"Would you change anything in here?"

She spun around slowly taking in the room fully. "If you wanted to add a bit of luxury, maybe add a fireplace. Gas."

He made a face. "Wood burning."

"Not practical. Besides, if it were…I mean, if you had a…" *Stop and shut up or speak as if what you're saying is no big deal.* She'd try to shut up and see if it worked. She picked at imaginary lint on the front of her coat. She really needed to get out more and learn how to be around hot men so she didn't make a fool of herself.

"What's that?" Clearly, by the way he was looking at her, not finishing her thoughts was not an option.

She tapped her finger against her chin and looked at the spot on the wall, behind his shoulder, hoping it would look like she was staring at him directly. "I was saying that if um, there were a woman in here, maybe she wouldn't want to be bothered starting a fire and it would just be easier to flick a switch."

He didn't say anything for a second and she had to look, and then swallowed hard. There was that expression on his face that made her wonder…of course he'd never had feelings for her. "What would you want?"

Her mouth dropped open slightly and she felt a heat swim up through her clothes. She adjusted the wool scarf around her neck, fighting the urge to rip it off because it suddenly felt as though it were choking her. She was an idiot. Her mouth was parched and she felt as though she were standing in the middle of the desert, dehydrated and overheated.

"I mean, since you're a woman."

Oh, see? No feelings for her. She was overreacting. He was just being a practical guy. She cleared her throat after she attempted speaking and ended up squawking. "I'd want gas. Besides, you already have a wood burning fireplace in the other room. I'd get a realistic one for sure. You can still get a rustic wood mantle. I'd get an open fire pit, definitely don't cover it up with glass or anything like that."

He gave a slow nod. "I'll consider it, but I don't like it," he said with a small half-grin.

"Well, someone else might thank me," she said, looking at the mountains in the distance instead of him. She was an idiot. She didn't want to think about some random woman thanking her for the romantic night she spent in Chase's new house, with his new gas fireplace—

"There's no one, Jules."

She didn't say anything. She didn't want to think of him as alone or lonely, but she didn't want to think of him with anyone else. Then again, what did that mean since she wasn't planning on staying here? She never wanted a family again. Chase was a family man. So, basically it was a lose-lose situation.

"We should go see the other two bedrooms," she said, pointing to the hallway. Time to get out of here and focus, meditate or something. She needed to stop thinking of him in any other way than a friend. Chase had been Michael's best friend and as much as she hated to even think about it, he might have known about Michael's…extracurricular activities. She also couldn't contemplate being a mother again, and Maggie needed a mother, a whole one, not this damaged, guarded version of a mother that she'd be able to offer. She had created a new life for herself, away from Shadow Creek, and she was fully intending on returning to it after the holidays.

The rest of the house tour seemed much less eventful after that, and almost as if a distance came between them. She was fine with that, because she needed to get her feelings under control. She hadn't expected any of this. They stood at the entry, Chase's hand on the doorknob. "I want to do this. I want this house for me and Maggie, and I want to be in here by Christmas. I want this Christmas to really be ours."

She took a deep breath, her heart squeezing as his love for his little girl was obvious in every word, every effort he made. "Okay. Then let's get the papers signed and I'll present the offer to Marlene this afternoon. Why don't we set this offer on the kitchen counter, talk numbers, and get some signatures?" she said, pulling out her portfolio with listing papers. "You and Maggie deserve this place. I'll call you tonight as soon as I have word. I won't give them a long time to decide."

"I'm in good hands," he said, his voice holding something delicious in it. She fumbled with the papers and they slid out onto the counter. She gathered them into a stack and straightened them out on the counter a few times, trying to regain her composure. She kept focused on the task at hand, remembering the reasons she'd just listed to herself why letting Chase close would be a mistake.

"Thanks. Are you still intent on keeping this a secret from Maggie?"

He nodded. "Yup. As soon as you tell me this place is ours, I'll drive her over here."

She smiled as she put the papers in order. "I think she's going to flip."

"I hope so."

"I'm sure…okay, here we go. Looks like I'm going to be presenting two offers to Marlene this afternoon."

"Oh yeah?"

She nodded, pointing at the spots he needed to sign. "Yup. Gwen and Lily want the old apothecary."

He didn't look up as he scrawled his name across the appropriate line. His hands were tanned, large, and his signature was bold and confident…and why was she even noticing this kind of thing? How many men had she given real estate offers to sign? "Good for them. You think you can get it for them?"

She took the signed copy and handed him another one. "Again, another case of Marlene pretending it's a high demand listing. No one has been through there in months. I'll see what I can get her to agree to. Anything will help them with the start-up expenses."

"I'm happy for Lily."

"Because of Jack you mean?"

He gave a short nod.

"Me too." She looked down at the stack of papers in her hand. "We both ran."

His hand covered hers and she tried not to jump at his warm touch. She stared down at his hand on hers. The feel of him sent a swirl of energy through her body. "You did what you had to do, babe."

Her eyes flew to his, her voice caught somewhere deep inside, and in a spot saved for dreams and desires she didn't dare think about during the day, but he was making it impossible to remember that long list of reasons she couldn't be with him. Babe. He'd never called her that, and yet it sounded perfectly natural coming from his mouth. She pulled her hand from his. "Thanks, but it's still up there with my biggest regrets."

His gaze was intense, his blue eyes focused on hers in a way that made her think he could know her better than anyone. "We all have regrets. Impossible to get through life without them. Can't go back and change that, but going forward you can prevent yourself from doing them again."

"So you're the county psychologist as well as sheriff?" She tried to lighten the mood and was rewarded by his deep, rich laughter.

He leaned against the counter, his face close to hers. Blue eyes, the color she always associated with the clear blue Montana sky, held hers so she couldn't look away. "Only for you. I hate talking to people."

This time she laughed. "That's not true."

He shrugged. "People tell you things you wished you never heard."

"Really? Like what?"

"Dustin Delaney's wife is cheating on him with Lorraine from the food market."

Her smile faltered at the mention of cheating. His smile fell a few seconds later. Did he know? Chase had been her rock, the good guy who'd been there for her. Though he'd technically been Michael's best friend, after the accident they'd become close. The thought that he knew the truth about Michael gutted her.

She tore her gaze from his and began filling in some of the blanks on the top of the offer page. "Okay then. Let's do this." She was going to do everything she could to get this place for Chase and Maggie, and she was not going to wonder about if he knew what his best friend had been up to, because that might be the last thing she could deal with right now.

Chapter Five

Julia smiled across the table at Gwen and Lily. They were seated in a booth at the Mountainside Inn, waiting for their drinks to be served. The Inn was a landmark in town, owned by the third generation Delaney family.

The main part of the Inn was a traditional log style home, but on a grand scale. There were outlying cabins scattered on the vast acreage, most of them with a view of the mountains. The main building had an impressive two story lobby and a dining room that spanned the length of the back of the Inn. Leather booths, wide-planked floors, and oversized hanging lanterns added a moody feel to the rustic dining room. Red poinsettias lined the bottom of the massive windows and an oversized pine wreath hung over the mantel of the floor to ceiling stone fireplace. White candles flickered in rustic lanterns throughout the room. It was Julia's favorite restaurant in Shadow Creek.

The week had passed by quickly and she'd been kept busy negotiating real estate deals with Marlene Mayberry. She was thrilled that the deal with Chase's house was so close to being finalized and now the deal for the chocolate shop was also finalized. She had been a go-getter in the city, pouring herself into her work. Being busy with work kept her from thinking about everything she'd lost, everyone back here in Shadow Creek. It had left her exhausted, unfulfilled, and empty, but that's all she'd wanted. She didn't take vacations or spend her money on luxury. She had put it all in the bank, never really caring about the numbers. She made large donations to her favorite charities, but didn't have anything else to spend her money on. Back here for two weeks, she already felt more fulfilled. She was helping people she loved move forward with their lives. She had also spent quite a bit of time with Chase. Sure, she had spent time with him in the past, but this was different…

"So this is really going to happen, isn't it?" Lily said, taking a sip of her red wine after their waiter had left with their dinner order.

"Yes! Let's toast to you both," Julia said, holding up her glass and smiling at her friends.

"And to you, best agent and sister-in-law *ever* who negotiated for free rent for three months for us against Marlene and won," Gwen said.

"You are so welcome," she said, taking a sip of her wine. "Okay, now that we're finally getting together and catching up, I want you to tell me what's going on in your lives. Tell me something good," she said. She had kept in touch with both of them, but she knew things were different now that she was back home. She wanted to use this time to get to know them again. She'd missed them more than she'd realized. Denial could convince a person of a lot of things.

"I would, except there's nothing. Absolutely nothing going on in my life," Lily said with a sigh.

Gwen reached for the wine and topped up her glass. "Yup. Nothing."

Julia leaned forward. She wasn't buying that for a second. "Come on, there has to be something."

Gwen gave her a pointed look and placed her wine glass back on the polished tabletop. "Well, neither of us have been seen around town with the hottest sheriff in the state."

Julia choked on her wine and they both laughed. "Chase and I are…friends."

Gwen rolled her eyes. "Right."

She crossed her arms and tried not to look suspicious. "Seriously."

"Why don't you spare us the agony of having to drag out the truth," Lily said, topping up her own glass.

Julia twirled the stem of her wine glass and focused her eyes on the roaring fire and thought of Chase. Well, she always thought of him, in so many different ways than she had before, but what was she supposed to say? She had a crush? Was she sixteen years old? "Okay, so the truth is I don't know what the truth is. I don't know…"

"Let me try and sum it up for you." Gwen took a deep, dramatic breath before continuing. "Both of you are attracted to each other and you're scared, and you think you're not going to stay in Shadow Creek so you don't want to start something."

Omigod. How did Gwen know all this? Julia blinked, trying to look as though she was contemplating what Gwen had just said.

"And stop pretending you don't already know this!"

Julia covered her face, her elbows on the table, and shook her head. "Fine," she said, her voice coming out muffled. "You're exactly right."

"I knew it!" Lily said.

Julia raised her index finger. "But I don't know what he thinks."

"I can tell you what he thinks," Gwen said.

Julia made a sweeping gesture with her hand. "Please do."

Gwen gave a nod. "Chase wants you."

Don't blush. Don't smile.

"Your smile and blush totally gave it away," Lily said, leaning forward.

"Hey, I hope you know everyone wants to see you happy. No one wants you to spend the rest of your life alone, sweetie. You're too young for that. And we all love Chase. He's like my third brother, just as irritating as my other two," Gwen said with a smile and gave her hand a squeeze.

Julia sunk down in the booth and groaned. "I know. Thank you. It's not…I don't know…I haven't dated anyone."

Lily leaned forward. "In five years? There was no one in the city? I mean, not that I'm judging, it's not like my personal life has been stellar, or even remotely hopeful."

Julia shook her head. "Nope. There were men, but none I was interested in."

"Ah, yes. So you mean there were no men like our rugged but tenderhearted and sensitive Sheriff Donovan," Gwen said, trying hard not to laugh.

"Are you the leader of his personal fan club? You're about as subtle as Marlene's makeup."

"Did I hear my name?"

Julia could have sworn they all gasped as they looked over at Marlene who was staring down at them, hands on her red, sequined-wrapped hips. Clearly, the woman hadn't heard her comment because she was grinning at them, her lips the same color as her glittering dress.

"Oh, Marlene, what a pleasant surprise." She didn't dare look over at either Gwen or Lily, but she did hear wine being choked on.

"Well, I do like to be unpredictable. It keeps my opponents guessing!" She reached inside her purse and pulled out a stack of papers. "I do think this is what I call fate. Now I don't have to go home and fax this signed offer to you. Tell the sheriff he drives a hard bargain," she said, slapping down the real estate offer.

Julia placed her hands on the stack of paper and slid it over and placed it on her lap. First off, she could practically feel the heat of Lily and Gwen's stares. Chase had sworn her to secrecy and now thanks to Marlene she was going to have to tell them about the house. But she was thrilled that this meant he was going to get the home. "So this is it? Your clients accepted?"

Marlene pursed her lips. "Yes, they did. It was wonderful doing business with you, dear. Just make sure we get the sheriff's signature on that ASAP before they change their mind."

Julia nodded, still avoiding eye contact with her friends. "I'll get that for you tonight."

Marlene nodded. "Excellent. Well, I must run. I have a business dinner. It's quite the demanding life being married to the most successful mayor in Shadow Creek history as well as being a real estate mogul. Being a power couple is so demanding!"

This time it was Lily who choked on her wine. Marlene didn't seem to notice.

"You're an inspiration to us all," Gwen said, lifting her glass in Marlene's direction.

Marlene's chest swelled. "Thank you, dear. We women have to stick together in business," she said with a fist pump on the table that sent the water in their glasses overflowing slightly.

"Ta-ta for now," she said, before twirling in a dizzying array of sparkles and perfume.

As soon as she was out of earshot they burst into uncontrollable laughter. After a few minutes, all attention was turned back to Julia. She shifted uncomfortably in her seat.

"Wow, I didn't think power couples actually referred to themselves as power couples, in public anyway," Julia said, hoping she would distract them by keeping the conversation on Marlene.

"All right. Spill it. Chase. Negotiations. You."

Julia rolled her eyes and tried to make it like there was so nothing going on. "She's exaggerating."

"Now," Lily said.

Lucky for her, their shared appetizers arrived and she sat quietly avoiding their intense stares as a platter of stuffed mushroom caps, spinach and artichoke dip and tortillas, and baked brie was placed in front of them.

"This looks so good," she said, busying herself with loading her plate.

Gwen grabbed her plate, laughing. "No food until all details are dished."

Julia sighed. The cat was out of the bag. She knew Chase wouldn't mind her saying anything, especially since the deal had gone through. "Okay, but you have to keep it quiet. He wants this to be a surprise for Maggie. Also? Hand me back that plate. I need that dip."

Gwen slid the plate across the table. She loaded up her tortilla and ate it while they filled their plates.

"Okay, so here's the deal. Chase wants a new house for the two of them and asked for my help."

Gwen smiled, her mushroom paused in the air, as though she had just received the answers to all of life's questions. "And you delivered?"

"It looks that way," she said, taking a long sip of wine before diving back into her food. She would go over there right after dinner and surprise him. She was also aware of how happy that made her, seeing him smile, being able to help him like this.

"So you've had to spend a lot of time with him these last

two weeks?"

She rolled her eyes and stabbed her fork into a mushroom. "Just as I have with you."

"Except she's not Chase," Lily said with a wink.

"And during that time things have been strictly platonic?"

"Of course."

"All right I'm going to cut to the chase, good one, isn't it? Everyone can see the chemistry you two have. Please tell me you're not going to ignore that."

"I will admit that Chase is…hot. And I will admit that I'm attracted to him on many levels. I love Maggie. But what's the point in any of that? In three weeks I'll be long gone. I can't get attached to him and I can't let Maggie get attached to me. Those two have had so much disappointment and it will kill me to hurt that little girl."

"What if you didn't go back?" Gwen said softly. "Don't you miss it here? I thought when you left it would be temporary, but I always pictured you coming back for good."

Julia finished the rest of her wine and tried to wash down the guilt and the ache that Gwen's words brought on. "I know. I've gotten used to my life out there."

"But you're all alone."

She shrugged. Alone, in a lot of ways, was easier. "I've gotten used to it."

"You're too young for that. Besides, if I had a man like Chase after me—"

"First off, Chase isn't after me."

"He's been after you since the night you came home. I saw the expression on his face when he hugged you and whispered something in your ear in that deliciously deep voice of his. He looked like he wanted to inhale you."

She poured the last of the wine from the bottle into her glass. "You've been reading way too many romance novels. 'Deliciously deep?'" Okay, so she wasn't about to admit that

that was the perfect description of his voice and that she remembered the shiver that had rushed through her when he'd whispered in her ear.

"That's actually what his voice sounds like," Lily added, not helping her at all.

"I think we're supposed to be talking about the improvements you wanted to make to your new unit," she said, sliding the file folder filled with design ideas she'd brought along with her across the table.

Gwen snatched it and slid it to the other end. "That can wait. What cannot wait is you admitting what you're really afraid of so that we can tell you not to be afraid and then convince you to stay."

She leaned back in her chair and eyed her sister-in-law, wondering if she'd always been this nosy. "I'm not afraid. I'm a realist."

Lily groaned. "Just talk. I can't take this torture anymore."

Julia rolled her eyes. "Nothing is happening. It's not just me. Neither of us are on the market."

"Chase is in the market. You're peering through the market doors and frankly if he is the produce, you should be adding him to your cart."

Julia stifled her laugh at Gwen's analogy. She couldn't encourage this.

"That man is like the finest piece of beef."

Julia held up her hand, choking on her wine. "You guys are ridiculous. What am I supposed to do? I'm not staying here. He doesn't need someone walking into their life only to leave in a few weeks."

"So that means if you weren't leaving in a few weeks this would be a possibility?"

She leaned back in her booth and stared at the pine boughs hung on the doorknobs. She couldn't keep denying that she had feelings. "Okay, fine. There *is* something there."

"Obviously."

"He deserves someone like you."

She folded and unfolded her napkin a few times. "What about other women in his life?"

"What women? After Sandy left that was it."

Her heart stopped for a second, thinking back to what he'd said at the house. She thought he meant there was no one now. Not…ever. "That was four years ago."

"Yup. That's not for want of trying from every single, and not so single, woman in the county, mind you," Gwen said. She pushed her plate away. "Okay, I need to stop eating."

"But this dip is *sooooo* good," Julia said, loading up another tortilla.

"The best in town. These are partly to blame for my twenty-pound weight gain," Gwen said with a laugh that didn't exactly sound funny.

"Don't start again," Lily said, dipping a chip into the creamy dip.

"Gwen, you look great," Julia said.

Gwen frowned at her. "Sure. Which is why I haven't been out with a guy in like…years. Years!"

Lily rolled her eyes. "It's not because of your weight."

Gwen wiped her mouth and frowned at the platters of food and then took another tortilla chip and dipped it in with a theatrical sigh. "Of course it is."

"Or maybe it's because you aren't confident anymore. You wear baggy clothes and are always making fun of yourself." Lily softened her words by placing her hand over Gwen's.

Gwen's eyes filled with tears but she waved her hand, complete with loaded tortilla, in front of her face. "Stop it." Globs of artichokes fell onto the tabletop as she spoke. "I know what I am and it's a problem."

Julia leaned forward. "I don't know why you're making it sound like you're so repulsive. You're gorgeous, Gwen. Big deal, you put on a few pounds."

Gwen rested her half-eaten chip down on her side plate. "Twenty."

Julia shrugged. "Yeah, so what? You wear them well."

Gwen rolled her eyes. "No one who is 5-5' can wear twenty extra pounds well."

"Stop, you're being ridiculous and way too hard on yourself."

"Really? Well, why didn't either of you put on any weight? You both had it just as hard. Julia even harder."

Julia rolled her eyes. "I couldn't eat. Besides, I think the problem is your parents. Since I've been back in town, what two weeks, I've gained five pounds!"

They all laughed.

"It's true. That house…after everything happened…I think we all turned to eating. I mean, the house was suddenly empty. Our lives were empty. It was just the three of us, night after night. Then Dad with the cancer. It was so depressing. All of it was overwhelming and I had no time for myself anymore to walk or work out. I was so focused on taking care of them that I forgot to take care of myself."

"You made them a priority, and you should be proud of that. Don't be so hard on yourself. I should have been around to help you out."

Gwen shook her head. "No, Jack should have been around."

The table went silent. She glanced over at Lily who was looking away. "Yes, he should have been around. Coming back home for Christmas is too little too late. I'm sorry, Gwen. I know you're all looking forward to him coming home."

"Don't apologize. If I were you, I'd be ready to strangle him the second he walks back into town."

Lily gave a little laugh that didn't really sound all that happy. She took a sip of her wine. "I might have to do that," she said, with an edge to her voice.

"How about you and I start walking in the morning before the day starts getting busy?" she said to Gwen. Her sister-in-law smiled and raised her glass to toast.

"Okay, let's do it. Here's to a great Christmas and fresh starts."

The three of them clinked their glasses.

"Now, enough about me. I'm supposed to be convincing you to take the plunge with Chase, and then move back to Shadow Creek."

Julia almost spilled the contents of her wine glass. "Oh, is that all?"

Gwen nodded. "Yep."

"Me too. Move back. Look how much fun we're having. We can do this every Friday night if you moved back. Tell me you met better friends back in the city?"

She tapped her index finger on her chin and tried to keep a straight face. "Well, there is Sarah and Theresa from the agency."

She burst out laughing when Gwen threw a bread bun in her face. Thankfully, it missed her wine glass. "Fine. Joking. Of course there was no one better than my two nosiest friends."

"And no better guy than Chase," Lily said, raising her glass.

"Very sneaky of you, already raising your glass."

"You're a tough one to fool."

She reluctantly raised her glass as well, hating that they were right. She glanced at her watch, her stomach flipping over gently at the thought of seeing Chase tonight.

Chapter Six

Chase stared at the white dishes in his hands and refused the urge to just chuck them in the trash can instead of washing them. It's not that he didn't do dishes. Hell, he'd been doing dishes since he was five and had learned the hard way that if you wanted something done in life, you had to do it yourself instead of waiting for someone else to do it for you. That was one of many lessons he'd learned at a young age, as the only child of two alcoholic parents.

His childhood had been a classic episode of *Hoarders*. It was why he hated clutter. He couldn't let dishes sit in the sink, couldn't let crap pile up around the house. The memory of his childhood home would flash in front of him every now and then and he had to remind himself that he would never have to live like that again. When he'd been old enough to realize he couldn't save people who didn't want to be saved, he'd walked out of that house, and never looked back.

Maybe that had been part of the reason he'd wanted to be a cop. He wanted to defend and protect the people that wanted safety and order. But every single time he got called out to a place with kids, it hit him on an emotional level, that even years of training and experience couldn't interfere with. He also knew people didn't really change. Had he felt guilt when he'd left his parents in search of a better life? Hell yes. That didn't change his life path, though. He'd been born with killer survival instincts.

Being around his parents made his gut churn, made him angry, made him feel worthless. He couldn't afford to let himself feel like that. He had a daughter who depended on him to be solid, engaged, and whole. He had citizens who needed him to be strong and fearless. He couldn't do that by having a relationship with people who didn't value him as a person, or as a son. As a father, he could never understand how his parents could have failed him on such a basic level. He would give the world to see that his little girl grew up in a happy, healthy, safe home. That was his biggest goal in life, to raise a girl that would one day be a strong, happy, independent woman.

Sandy leaving had sent him into a backward spiral, and it was only because of his desperation to raise his daughter differently than he'd been that had kept him from abusing the bottle. It was never far from his thoughts that he was always only a bottle or two away from following in his parents' footsteps. He'd read the stats on addiction being hereditary. He saved it for his worst nights and even then, his limit was two glasses. Sandy's leaving their family was a reflection on him. He still blamed himself for marrying someone so selfish and irresponsible. He would never be able to make that up to Maggie.

He glanced over in time to see Maggie bang her head against the kitchen table theatrically. "How's the homework going, Maggie?"

"It won't even be finished in time for Christmas," was the muffled reply.

"I'm sure you can get it done."

She lifted her head with a start, the gleam in her eye visible across the kitchen. "How about we have a race? Let's see who can finish first."

He pointed his index finger in her direction. "Deal, but no sloppy work. I'm still going to inspect it."

She nodded. "Same goes for you. I'll inspect how clean the kitchen is."

He chuckled. "Fair enough."

"Care to make a wager?"

He leaned his head back and laughed. He loved her competitive streak. "No gambling, remember?"

She frowned.

He ignored her. "Ready. Set. Go!"

Barely a second later her head was down, and her pencil was to the paper. They worked like that for the next half hour, while Christmas music from the radio kept them company. Of course, give him a moment where he actually had time to think, and his thoughts went to Julia. The way she'd been standing in that house the other day, telling him her design ideas. Had he been asking her what she'd want? Hell, yes. He wanted to know. Maybe it was childish, foolish of him to imagine her there with him, but he did. He knew in his gut they were meant to be together. Now all he had to do was prove it to her before she left for good this time.

The doorbell rang and Maggie was out of her chair before he could even dry his hands on the dishcloth, so he dried them on the front of his shirt and followed her out.

"It's Julia!" Maggie yelled as he stepped into the small entryway.

Sure enough, Julia was standing there, her cheeks rosy, her lips the color of her red scarf. Snow fell gently outside and she looked like a dream come true, standing there on his porch. She was smiling down at his little girl and his heart squeezed painfully at the sight. "Sorry I came by without calling, but I had some news and I was on my way home so I thought I'd drop by."

"You never have to call," his daughter said, beating him to it and then proceeded to yank Julia forward. He was laughing along with Julia as she entered the house.

"Thanks, Maggie. I love your Christmas lights out there," she said.

"That was Daddy. I just gave the orders," she said, taking Julia's coat and hanging it on a hook beside the door.

"Yeah. Maggie is about as bossy as I am, so I know I don't stand a chance arguing with her."

Julia laughed, the sound filling up the small entrance. He found himself checking her out without her coat on. She was wearing one of those cardigan things that didn't have buttons and was longer in the front. It looked soft and warm…much like the woman herself. Her dark jeans and the red shirt she wore under the cardigan hugged her curves.

"Come on in. I was about to put a pot of coffee on. Wanna cup?"

She walked forward, her arm around Maggie. "That would be great. It's freezing out there."

"I'm so glad you came. Daddy, does this mean I don't have to finish my homework?"

Chase chuckled at the hopeful look on his daughter's face. "Uh, nice try, but nope. Besides, I thought you were going to win the race?"

Maggie scrunched up her nose. "All bets are off due to interference."

"Contest?" Julia asked.

Maggie nodded while he took out the coffee grinds and prepped the coffee. "Daddy and I were bored. I didn't want to do my homework, because it's soooooo boring, and he didn't want to do dishes so we thought we'd have a contest."

"That's a great idea. But I interrupted?"

"That's okay. I was going to win," she said with a wink. Julia burst out laughing and he stood there wondering when his daughter had turned eight going on eighteen.

"What are you working on?" Julia asked. Maggie pulled on her hand and they sat side by side at the table while he waited for the coffee to brew.

"Math, which is *so* boring."

"Oh I used to think so too. How much do you have left?"

"Five more questions! And then it'll be bedtime! It's like our teacher is the Grinch's wife." Maggie banged her head on her textbook dramatically once again.

He made eye contact with Julia who was covering her mouth, her eyes narrowed with laughter. He shook his head and leaned against the counter. He wasn't even going to let himself think how perfect this was, Julia here, the three of them on this winter's night, just hanging out like a family. God, this is what he always wanted—a good woman, a woman he loved, desired. A child. This is what he'd wanted since he'd figured out that good families really existed. He fisted his hands and forced his eyes away from the perfect picture the two of them made at the table. Instead he looked out the window and cursed himself for still wanting things that the boy inside him wanted. He knew better. He'd lived through shit and he'd seen shit, so wanting so much more was futile. It was juvenile to wish for things.

"Okay, how about this? If you hurry up and get through this, I can read you a bedtime story?"

His drama queen daughter lifted her head, looking like a new kid. She spread her arms wide. "Deal. Nobody talk to me."

Julia stood as he walked over with two mugs of coffee. "How about we go into the living room and give Maggie peace and quiet while she works?"

"Perfect. I'm going to grab my file and I'll meet you there," she said, walking out of the room.

He followed her out, telling himself he shouldn't be checking her out from behind, even though it was a great view. He placed the mugs down on the coffee table and turned on a table lamp. Julia was back in a moment and sat on the couch. He sat down beside her. The room was quiet except for the low sound of Christmas music playing from the kitchen.

"Do you still take your coffee with milk, no sugar?"

She nodded, reaching for her cup. "Good memory. Yes, this is perfect," she said, taking a sip. "Okay. So I didn't want to say anything in front of Maggie, but you got it, Chase."

He put his cup down on the table and slowly stood. "What?"

She looked up at him, and emotion clogged his throat as she sat there, smiling at him.

"The house. You got it," she whispered, standing up. He reached for her hand and tugged her into him and suddenly she was wrapped in his arms, and everything felt right. He remembered everything about holding her. Even though he hated thinking of that time in their lives, he remembered how she felt, how she smelled, how she fit him so perfectly.

"Thank you," he said, his voice sounding hoarse to his own ears.

She cleared her throat and slowly pulled back. His hands dropped to his sides and he saw the fear in her eyes, the reservation.

"You're welcome," she said and sat down, quickly grabbing her coffee. She grabbed the file. "I'm so happy for you, and for Maggie. This will be the best Christmas present ever," she whispered, glancing out the hallway.

He reached for his coffee and settled back into the cushions with a sigh. He couldn't push Julia. He didn't want to scare her. He forced himself to focus on the reason she came by—not on his own feelings. "How did you manage to get Marlene to agree to all our terms?"

She lifted a brow and gave him a little smirk that he found incredibly adorable as she flipped open the file. "I called her on the fact that there was no interest in the place. I may have also suggested you were too busy for going back and forth and that if we couldn't close this deal in the next twenty-four hours you were going to stay put in this house and not move at all."

He grinned. "That's brilliant."

"Thanks. I thought so. I just really, really wanted this for you and Maggie. That house is perfect."

"I think so."

"So, they agreed to everything?"

She eyed him over the rim of her mug and took a sip. "Yup. Since there's no financing conditions, this can move really quickly. If you can get that building inspection done in the next day or two, that's all we need."

Julia flipped through the offer agreement and then presented him with three sheets that had sticky notes attached to the sides. "I need your signature and initials on these pages." She slid the papers over to him and he took the pen from her, feeling the slight tremor in her hand as it brushed against his. Once finished, she took the papers and efficiently lined them up and placed them neatly back in her file.

"We're done. I'll fax this over to Marlene tonight."

"Thanks, Jules." He took a sip of coffee and crossed his ankle over the other. He didn't want her to leave yet.

"So, when are you going to tell Maggie?" Julia whispered, glancing over her shoulder before speaking.

He grinned. "Maybe tomorrow morning. If I tell her now she'll never go to sleep," he said with a low chuckle. "When can we list this place?"

"I can get the sign on your lawn tomorrow afternoon. I

think it'll go quickly despite the season. It's right downtown, updated, and affordable."

He was nodding as she spoke. "Do you have listing papers for this house?"

"I come prepared," she said, flipping through her briefcase and then pulling out a fresh listing agreement.

She worked in silence until it was time to discuss numbers. He knew enough about the local real estate market that agreeing on a price was quick and painless.

"So you're good with this listing price?"

He nodded. It was exactly what he'd thought it was worth. He'd known how to manage money from an early age. Growing up with nothing forced a person to learn how to be frugal, and he had been when he was starting out. He'd worked two jobs before Maggie had been born. He'd used the money from the one job and put it directly into savings. The other went to living expenses. Of course after Maggie everything had changed, but he'd already had a solid amount of savings. Since Sandy had walked out on him, he wasn't paying her a dime, which was fine with him, since he was the one providing for their kid. He was in a decent financial position. That filled him with pride when he thought back to what he came from. He was able to provide his little girl with a comfortable life, and now a nice house with a big yard to play in. He wanted to give her the childhood he never had.

By the time they finished, their coffees were done and it was late.

"I can't wait for her to find out."

"Find out what?"

She jumped in her seat. Maggie was standing in the doorway, hands on her hips, mischievous grin on her face.

"You know Christmas isn't a time for being nosy and asking questions," Chase said, trying to keep a straight face.

She rolled her eyes and shrugged. "It was worth a try."

"Are you finished with your homework?"

She threw her arms in the air. "Done!"

"I should probably check it over," he said, rising.

"It's on the table. I'm sure it's perfect. I'm going to get my pajamas on so Auntie Julia can tuck me in and read me a Christmas book. Call me if there's a problem," she said before walking out of the room.

Julia burst out laughing. "Wow. That's totally your daughter. She's good at giving orders, but her charm keeps her from sounding bossy."

"So you're saying I'm charming and bossy, but I hide it well."

She stood, picking up her empty mug. The look in her eyes beckoned him. She was fighting the attraction. He knew she was scared. Hell, he couldn't blame her. But he also knew that if she left Shadow Creek without knowing how he really felt about her, he'd regret it. He'd never been one to run scared. He took a step closer to her, and he watched the emotions play across her expressive eyes. She didn't move back, but she didn't move forward either.

"Chase," she whispered.

"Yeah?" he said, swallowing the last bit of air between them. He lifted his hands to her hair, slowly moving his hand to cup the nape of her neck.

"We shouldn't be doing any of this," she whispered, raising her eyes to his.

He stilled. "Why not?"

She licked her lips. "Because I'm going home after Christmas. We can't start something that will go nowhere. I can't leave here with a broken heart twice."

"Then don't leave," he whispered gruffly.

She closed her eyes for a moment and he leaned down to kiss her lids. The softest, sexiest whimper came from her parted lips and she clutched his arms. He slowly pulled back and she opened her eyes and God, when her gaze went from his eyes to his lips he knew he had to kiss her. He could see the pulse at the base of her throat beating rapidly and her lips were parted, her breath hitched.

It wasn't the first time tonight he'd noticed her lips. They always looked so damn kissable, with that lower one larger than the top. He'd fantasized about tugging on it, kissing it, her, until both of them forgot everything they were both afraid of.

"I can't do that. I have to leave. This isn't my home anymore."

"You can try again."

She shook her head. "I can't. I can't risk it all again. For anyone," she said, taking a step back from him. It was only a step, but it felt as though she'd just put up a massive stone wall between them.

"I'm not going to tell you what you should be feeling or what you should be doing, but I can tell you that sometimes it's worse to try and bury what you're feeling because sometimes what you feel becomes so strong and powerful it becomes impossible to ignore. Sometimes it can be all-encompassing. All you think about. All you want, day and night."

Everything in her eyes told him she felt every ounce of desire he did, and it humbled him. It affected him profoundly because this was the woman he'd wanted for a lifetime and everything he felt for her was staring him back in the eyes. Except for the fear, which was why he didn't move.

He didn't take it personally. He knew she was afraid. He shoved his hands in his back pockets. Her mouth parted again, and the heat and longing in her eyes was almost enough to make him want to walk across and kiss her until he convinced her with his mouth that he was worth the risk, but he wasn't going to do that. Julia would have to come to him. It was his job to make her want to take the risk. If it took a few more weeks then that was fine.

They stood in silence, the glow from the fireplace highlighting the rugged lines of his face, the emotion, the desire in his eyes.

"Auntie Julia! I'm all done!"

Julia jumped at the sound of Maggie. "On my way, Maggie." Julia scrambled, bumping into the sofa.

"I'll go check her homework and then be up to say good night," he said, as she left the room.

"Okay," she said. Her voice sounded squeaky as she practically flew out of the room.

He wasn't going to grin, but he was pretty damn happy that he could make her that flustered.

• • •

Julia closed *Rudolph* and glanced over at Maggie. Maggie was smiling, at her, looking so much like her father.

"I love that book, don't you?"

Julia nodded. "It was one of my favorites when I was little." Sometimes she wondered how she could remember pieces of her childhood so vividly and at the same time have trouble remembering life in Shadow Creek. She wondered if it was her mind's way of protecting her. She remembered Matthew with great detail, but sometimes she thought she *felt* more than she actually remembered. Matthew evoked feeling.

Now, in Chase and Maggie's home, those feelings returned. They rose to a surface she wasn't sure she was capable of holding down.

Chase had made it clear downstairs that he had feelings for her. She couldn't deny hers. She knew it was more than attraction, because she'd been around attractive men. Okay, maybe none as attractive as him, but still. He got her on another level, one that scared her, one that no one had ever really understood her on. The emotions were the problem now, because they were winning over logic. She wanted everything he was offering. She wanted to walk right into his arms and she wanted him to hold her and touch her without an ounce of sympathy, only desire. She wanted to remember what it felt like to be loved. She wanted to know what it felt like to be loved by Chase.

"Julia?"

She focused her attention back on the little girl who was staring at her with an intensity that matched her father's. "Yes, sweetie?"

"Do you know what Daddy's surprise is?"

She smiled as she rose from the bed, tucking the pastel quilt around Maggie. "I do."

"You're not going to tell me, are you?"

She laughed at the disgruntled look on her face. "Sorry. Your dad would kill me. This is his surprise. But I will tell you this, I think you're going to love it."

Maggie gave a nod and then a wide-mouthed yawn. "You're still coming to the pageant, aren't you?"

"Of course! I wouldn't miss that for anything."

Maggie smiled. "I'm glad. We've been rehearsing every day after school."

"Well, not much longer now. Five days?"

Maggie nodded. "I think this is going to be the best Christmas ever, Julia."

Julia's heart squeezed and then she leaned down and kissed Maggie's forehead. She had trouble holding on to her tears, the emotion that coursed through her, enveloping her in a cloud of warmth, want for this life that Chase and Maggie had. All her years of being away, protecting herself from emotion, only to be led here, right in the center of it all. She didn't know what was scarier—the thought of staying in it, exposing herself, or leaving.

Chapter Seven

Julia took off her red glove and knocked on the front door. She could have sworn she heard crying, but she couldn't be sure. Chase and Maggie were supposed to pick her up, but after a series of tense-sounding texts from Chase, she had volunteered to come over to their place. He'd hinted at some sort of imminent meltdown. From Maggie, not him.

The door swung open and she tried to hide her laugh at the image in front of her. Chase was standing there, in his go-to, hot, low-slung jeans and a T-shirt that seemed to hug the clearly defined lean, muscular lines of his shoulders and torso. And he was holding a curling iron. There was also panic in his eyes.

"Thank God you got here," he said, ushering her inside.

"What's this? Our calm, cool sheriff looking frazzled?"

He put the barrel of the curling iron to his temple as somewhat theatrical crying from upstairs trailed down the hallway. "Do you know how to use one of these things?"

"For suicide attempts or hairstyling?"

"You're cute when you're mocking me," he said, an

unmistakable glint in his eyes.

She wasn't going to blush like a school girl because he'd called her cute. Seriously, because she was old. Well, old-*ish* for blushing like that. She handed him her coat and was self-conscious in her red sweater dress and knee-high black boots. It wasn't that the dress was overly revealing, it was the way he looked at her. Not that he was ogling, because a man like Chase didn't need to ogle. No, he just needed to do a sweeping glance with those gorgeous blue eyes of his, a subtle clenching of that perfect, hard jaw and she was a wreck. This mutual attraction thing was not going to make her life easier. The fact that she'd been self-conscious of the weight she'd put on since being back in Shadow Creek was immediately erased by the obvious praise in his eyes.

"Daddy! We need to call and cancel! I can't be seen like this. I look like the Abominable Snowman in *Rudolph*!"

"Uh oh, what have you done?" Julia whispered to him.

Chase dragged his hands down his face and she could have sworn she heard him mutter, "May God help me" but she couldn't be sure.

She stifled her laugh. "Can I help?"

"Auntie Julia, is that you?"

Maggie appeared at the top of the stairs and Julia covered her mouth in order to muffle her gasp. The poor child looked as though she'd been electrocuted, her hair was standing at odd ends, her eyes wide and brimming with tears. "Oh dear God, Chase, don't tell me you're responsible for this," she hissed at him, torn between laughing and crying.

He gave her a level stare. "Can you fix it?"

"Give me half an hour," she said, holding out her hand.

He placed the curling iron in it and she marched up the stairs, filled with purpose. "Maggie, honey, don't worry. I'm going to help you. We'll get that hair all smoothed out and into shiny curls in no time, okay, sweetie?"

Maggie went from almost crying to beaming by the time she reached her at the top of the stairs. She gasped when she entered the washroom and saw the disaster zone that used to be a countertop.

"I feel really bad for getting mad at Daddy. I know he was trying his best, but this head is the type of thing nightmares are made of."

Julia laughed as she began combing Maggie's dark hair. She stood behind her while Maggie sat in a chair positioned in front of the mirror. "Well, it was pretty nice of him to try, wasn't it?"

Maggie nodded vigorously, her expression changing as Julia made eye contact with her in the mirror. "It was. He knows nothing about hair or fashion, but it's not his fault. He tries really hard to help me. He brushes my hair every night and every morning before school. Once in grade one I asked him if he could do a braid for me and he said he didn't know how. And I begged and begged because my best friend always had the nicest braids. The next morning he brought his laptop to the kitchen table and told me to sit down. He googled 'braid' and then tried to do one!"

Julia's heart squeezed at the image of Chase trying to make his little girl happy. "What happened?"

Maggie lowered her voice, but a few giggles escaped and Julia had to pause brushing her hair. "Well, he didn't think I heard, but he kept swearing under his breath because he ended up tying my hair in giant knots and still couldn't figure it out, even with all the pictures!"

They both burst out laughing. An amused noise startled her and she caught Chase's reflection in the mirror. He was leaning against the doorjamb, arms crossed over his wide chest, a smile across his face. "You couldn't possibly be laughing at me, could you?"

"No, Daddy. We love you so much, but don't quit your

day job!"

Julia thought she was going to die of laughter and the sound of Chase's deep laugh filled her with a peace she hadn't felt in a long time. The three of them, laughing and being together, made her remember what that sense of belonging, that easy feeling of being comfortable, felt like. It had been a long time.

"Thanks for the advice," Chase said, pushing off the door. "I guess I should get ready. I'll meet you two downstairs in ten minutes."

Julia nodded, grasping a small section of Maggie's fine hair and placing it in the iron.

Chase was watching intently and she wrapped it around the barrel. "Huh."

"It's okay, Sheriff, I got this," she said with a wink.

The look he gave her stole her breath away. She remembered him when they were young; his smile was exactly the same. There were glimpses she'd had of him, clues that had told her he'd be someone someday, but never this. Never a man this good.

As they'd grown up and each gotten married, he'd never ceased to impress her. And of course, she'd have to be blind to not notice that he was an extremely attractive man. Maybe on some level she'd always felt something for him, but she'd never allowed herself to go there. She had never been fond of Sandy; she'd always seemed immature, spoiled. But she was gone. Michael was gone.

It was just the two of them left. There had been so many times in the last five years that she mourned the man that she had thought loved her. She mourned the end of their marriage by herself. She had to face his betrayal on her own, without ever getting answers from Michael. She didn't want his parents to know, it would devastate them and they'd been through enough. Her in-laws had lost all of them five years ago. Little Matthew had been their pride and joy and they'd doted on him, taking him out to dinner, having him over for sleepovers, and they had treated her like a daughter. No, it wasn't fair to burden them. She had dealt with it.

Julia finished the last section of hair and then smoothed out a few flyaway pieces. She placed her hands on Maggie's shoulders and looked at her in the mirror and smiled. "What do you think?"

"I love it. Thank you, Auntie Julia!"

They met Chase at the front door; he was all dressed in uniform and Julia had to tear her eyes away from him, because of how good he looked. He was hard lines and admirable strength and she found it hard to breathe, and harder to ignore the feelings he brought out in her.

Ten minutes later they were walking the downtown. Julia paused for a moment, taking in the picturesque town on this particular night. It was her favorite night of the year. The downtown core of Shadow Creek was magical during the Christmas festival. Lights twinkled from the trees and storefronts. Wreaths on lampposts glowed with red bows and white lights. Carolers filled the air with lively Christmas carols. There was a hot chocolate booth in front of the town square and families were strolling and chatting. The stores were all open late, cedar roping draped over the windows, twinkling lights strung. Horse-drawn wagons with jingling bells trotted down the main street. How many years had she attended the Christmas festival night in Shadow Creek? But never had she attended with Chase. She looked up at him, and a part of her felt the need to reach out and take his hand in hers. She wanted to know what it would feel like to walk with him.

As though he knew she was looking at him, his gaze snapped to her. "It's good to have you here with us tonight," he said in that deep voice that made her insides warm.

"There's my class!" Maggie yelled, tugging on his arm.

"Can I go?"

"Sure, we'll go and get a seat," Chase said. "Have fun, Maggie."

"I will!" she yelled, before running off to join her classmates standing beside the large outdoor stage.

Julia took a deep breath of the cold winter air, trying to rein in the emotions that ploughed through her, pushing her from the present moment and into the past; the last time she was at the Christmas Festival. Michael and her sweet baby were alive. Matthew's eyes had been wide and curious, squeals of excitement erupting from his mouth as she pushed him in his stroller.

"You okay?" Chase whispered in her ear.

The sound of his deep voice, thick with concern, pulled her back into the present. She looked up at him, a slight frown across his brow, but it was the warmth in his eyes that appealed to her. Chase could be all hard lines and tough man, but the man had the softest core and she knew she was one of the few that was on the receiving end of it. She didn't breathe for a moment, his face close to hers. Her gaze lingered on his mouth and for a second she wished he'd kiss her. She knew, in her gut, that Chase kissing her would make her forget everything else. When was the last time she'd wanted a man to kiss her? Five years was a long time.

She cleared her throat and looked away when she realized she was staring. She pointed to the stage in the center of the park. "We'd better get a seat. Maggie will kill us if we don't get one near the front." She tried not to cringe at the squeaky sound of her voice. When had she become so obvious? Nothing could ever happen between her and Chase. She would be leaving Shadow Creek in a few weeks. He had a daughter. Neither of them could enter into a casual relationship. She had no choice but to get it together.

"Let's go," he said, taking her hand in his. A shiver raced

through her even though she was bundled up and warm. It was him. Having him hold her hand effortlessly, as though he'd been doing this for years. People stopped and chatted with Chase and he was polite and charming, flashing that smile of his easily. The town loved him and he was so at home here. Gwen, Cassy, and Edward were waving to them from the second row. Gwen gave her a pointed stare and raised her eyebrow high as she joined their row. Julia avoided eye contact with her. She knew to expect a barrage of texts as soon at the night was over. "They always get the best seats," Chase said.

Once they were settled, the crowd quickly filled in the remaining seats. Julia smiled as the stage curtains moved and small feet poked out beneath.

"There's always a badass back there that sneaks a peak through the curtain. And ten bucks says it's a boy," he said in her ear. She laughed, just as a dark haired little boy poked his head out.

Within minutes the performance started and the sound of children singing "Jingle Bells" filled the night sky. Tears pricked her eyes at the sweet sound of their voices and her heart felt full, her chest ached and she wasn't sure she'd be able to take a deep breath. As though he knew, Chase took her hand in his and rested on her leg. She didn't feel as alone, as solitary in her thoughts. He knew. He knew what she was thinking. Matthew would have been here tonight; she'd be watching him sing. How would he look now? What would his sweet voice have sounded like? It was so hard to imagine because in her mind he was always two. She had been blessed with the memory of him saying "mama" and she'd never forget it. Her heart swelled painfully, her body filled with shivers, goose bumps.

"You okay?" Chase whispered.

She nodded rapidly and then looked over at him while

the crowd clapped as the first number ended. Her breath caught in her throat at the look in his eyes. "I'm okay. I'm having a great time. I can't wait to see Maggie's class," she said, blinking back tears and looking straight ahead. She meant it. No matter what she was feeling, the memories she was battling, it was so good to be back here with everyone, to see Maggie here tonight.

They had to wait for two more classes to finish their songs and then finally Maggie appeared. She stood center stage and Chase sat up a little straighter. She glanced over at him and he was sitting there with unmistakeable pride stamped on his handsome face. The class began a singing and dancing number, some of the kids struggling to stay coordinated with the others. One boy almost fell off the stage and the crowd gasped, but he managed to regain his balance. They all stood and clapped, laughing when the number was over. "You can't get theater like this in the city," Chase whispered in her ear.

She laughed as they filed out of their seats.

"Are you coming to the tree lighting after?" her mother-in-law asked as they filed out.

"Yes, I think I'll go with Chase to pick up Maggie backstage. I promised her," Julia said. She noticed that Cassy looked extra happy with that news.

"That's very nice, dear," she said, patting her on the shoulder and all but pushing her into Chase. Apparently the entire family was encouraging this. She shouldn't be surprised. She knew her in-laws wanted her to be happy and she knew they wanted the same for Chase and Maggie. God, how she didn't want to disappoint any of them when she left town again.

They made their way through the crowd, Chase's hand linked in hers, and she wondered how it felt so natural. She didn't pull away. How could she? She was discovering him on a whole new level and while it was purely a friendly gesture, she felt it in a much more profound way. He had to stop every now and then and speak with people, and she noticed the curious glances some gave her.

"Julia, Julia, you certainly get around town!"

Julia forced a smile on her face as Marlene stopped them in the crowd. She heard Chase's sigh.

"Marlene, you have the funniest way of welcoming people." He softened his statement by laying on one of his charm-the-pants-off-a-woman smile.

"I guess what I meant to say was that I didn't realize she was out and about with you, Sheriff Donovan."

Chase squeezed her hand and his smile tightened. "Well, we're just two friends enjoying my daughter's play and the Christmas festival."

She waved an arm around. "Of course, of course. It was wonderful and little Maggie is adorable. It's so nice to see the both of you. We really have missed you, Julia. After the tragedy…well, it broke all our hearts to lose you too."

Julia swallowed and spoke up before Chase felt he needed to jump to her defense again. "Thank you, Marlene. It's good to be home. Shadow Creek is always home to me."

"Perhaps it could be again! We could even work together," she said, leaning forward, her oversized Christmas tree chandelier earrings dangling with the motion. "Look what we accomplished in the short time you've been back. Think about it. You could join my brokerage."

She could have sworn she heard Chase groan.

She smiled. "That's always something to think about, thank you so much for thinking of me. Nice to see you. I guess we'll chat about those offers tomorrow."

"You've got it, Missy. I'll buy you a coffee and we can talk business. We have to make sure the sale goes smoothly so our beloved sheriff gets his dream house for his little girl…and maybe start a family again. That house definitely has more than enough room."

"Well, we'd better get moving in case Maggie gets scared that we've forgotten to pick her up," Chase said, ushering her away. She swallowed her laugh as they walked toward the stage.

"She's still your favorite person, isn't she?" she asked him, trying to keep a straight face.

He gave her a smile that made her heart skip a beat. "Right up there with my ex."

She laughed.

"Daddy! Julia!" Maggie yelled as they rounded the outdoor stage. She came running up to them and hugged a leg on each of them.

She dangled her head back, while still holding on to them. "Was it the best play you've ever seen?"

Chase laughed. "Of course."

"Did you like it, Auntie Julia?"

"I loved it. You were great, honey."

Maggie beamed. "And are you going to stay for the tree lighting? You're not going to leave now, are you?"

The fear that was stamped across Maggie's little face tugged at her heart. How many people had left her life? "Of course I'm staying. I'll be around for the next few weeks, until after the holidays so we don't have to worry about that, okay?"

Maggie nodded, her shoulders relaxing. "Okay. Let's go," she said, grabbing each of their hands. Carolers were still strolling the sidewalks and the stores were bustling as they walked toward the town square. The giant tree was already surrounded by a small crowd waiting for the official lighting. She still remembered the expression on Matthew's face when he'd been here when he was two. The exact moment the tree went from dark to a magical brightly colored beauty. He'd squealed and clapped his hands. She remembered the full feeling in her heart at the sound. Her heart had never been as full as those days since before the accident. She doubted it ever could be again.

As the carolers' singing filled the air, she stood beside Chase and Maggie and waited. When the tree was finally lit, all the children clapped. Maggie beamed up at her, still holding her hand. That familiar feeling crept back, that feeling that only a child could bring. The innocent, unabashed happiness that a child had. She hadn't been back here long and she was already starting to feel things again. If she wasn't careful, the next few weeks were threatening to open up her heart again, and then where would she be when it was time to go home? She would not leave here broken-hearted again.

Half an hour later, they were standing by her rental car. Maggie was having a hot chocolate with the Baileys while Chase walked her back to her car.

"Thanks for helping with the hair debacle," he said with a half-grin.

"My pleasure. I arrived in the nick of time, I think."

"I was getting pretty suicidal, yeah," he said and she laughed out loud.

"What was Maggie's reaction when you told her about the new house?"

He stuffed his hands in his pockets. "She was a little concerned at first but then when I told her all about the new place and how it's the perfect house to make new memories and a fresh start, she got excited."

She smiled. "That's sweet. I think she'll be so happy. There's so much room to play and I love the room that will be hers—with the big windows overlooking the backyard. Perfect."

"I'm sure by the time I'm done taking orders from her it will resemble a pink and white candy cane."

She laughed. "You're probably right."

Snowflakes tumbled out of the sky lazily, adding a magical addition to the festival. White flecks clung to Chase's dark hair and her voice caught in her throat when he took a step closer. They were on a deserted side street, surrounded by quiet houses, the noise from the festival muted and in the distance.

She wanted to know if he knew the truth about Michael. She wanted to know because Chase had been her ally since the accident. He symbolized honor and loyalty, and it would kill her if he'd known, and it would kill the feelings she'd developed for him, not that she was willing to act on those feelings…but it was important for her to know.

"Thanks for being here, Jules," he said in that deep voice. His eyes held something in them that made her toes curl and as he reached out to hold her hand she said a silent prayer that he was the man she hoped he was. She needed to know that good guys still existed, that there were still people out there that were actually what they claimed to be.

"Thanks for inviting me," she said, her voice sounding breathy to her own ears. Of course, it was probably because he was standing inches from her, his large hand wrapped around hers, and she was imagining what it would be like if he leaned down and kissed her. Oh, God, she was setting herself up for disaster because she knew he'd be as good as she'd always imagined, but she shouldn't give in. Or if she did give in…well, one kiss didn't have to mean something. It wasn't a marriage proposal. It didn't have to change anything…just one.

"I mean, I'm glad you're home, in Shadow Creek, and I'm glad you're here, with me. I'm not a guy who wastes time wishing for things, but if I were, I wish you'd stay."

She hadn't expected that candor. She looked away from his intense gaze for a moment. "I don't…I haven't thought about it. It feels good to be back and of course see all of you. But I can't promise something that I know isn't going to happen," she whispered. She saw the unmistakable flicker of disappointment in his blue eyes, along with something else. It was the something else that made her stomach quiver.

"Hm," he said, swallowing up the last step between them, and any chance she had at ever being able to breathe normally again. Chase this close to her, with a heated look in his gaze was completely overwhelming—in the most wonderful way possible. "I wonder if I can convince you before the holidays are over that you should make this your home again."

She didn't answer his question because he'd reached out to frame the sides of her face with his hands, and frankly she was a wreck. His face was inches from hers, and her eyes seemed to not be taking any orders from her brain to not look at his mouth. It was a gorgeous mouth, and she knew he would know exactly what to do with his mouth. Omigod she was acting like a teenager, a teenager who'd never been kissed.

"Chase," she whispered, finally able to talk. She needed to know. She had to have an answer before he kissed her, because then it'd be even harder to walk away from him.

"Yeah?" he said, his gaze going from her mouth to her eyes.

"I...did you know that Michael was cheating on me?"

Chapter Eight

Hell. What. The. Hell?

Chase felt his body go from burning hot to cold in five seconds flat. He dropped his hands from Julia's face and took in her insecure expression. He knew she wasn't a liar. He would never question that, but the idea of what she was saying…it was impossible. He jammed his hands into his pockets and replayed her question in his head. Michael had been cheating?

"Cheating? Michael?"

She nodded and her eyes filled with a wariness and vulnerability that made his gut churn. She wanted to know if he was as big an ass as his best friend. God, if Michael were alive he'd kill him. He still remembered feeling so jealous of him when he went on his first date with Julia. He thought Michael had it all, and then when they'd gotten married, and then when Matthew was born. He had never let himself think he was a good enough man for Julia.

But it turns out his best friend had been even worse.

"Did you know, Chase?"

He shook his head. "No. Hell, no. God, no."

She closed her eyes for a moment and her shoulders slumped slightly. He bent his knees to look at her, eye level, and held her arms gently. "Are you sure? When did you know?"

She took a deep breath and then looked up into the sky. "After I moved. When I finally was able to go through his computer. I was looking for banking information and retrieving files that I would need. I noticed a string of emails from a lawyer whose name I recognized. He'd talked about her a lot in that last year. I stupidly didn't think anything of it." She paused and her chin wobbled and she adjusted her hat, before looking down at her boots. He struggled to remain calm and not demand all the answers. He was also struggling with his own need to pound his fist through a wall at the thought of what Michael had done. It wasn't fair. How could he have done that to her? She'd had to deal with all of this alone? All these years?

"What happened, sweetheart?"

Her head shot up and the tears were gone this time. "They…this woman and him had been seeing each other for about a year."

He bit back a few of his favorite expletives. "You know this for sure?"

She crossed her arms in front of her. "Yup. There were texts that I found. Oh, they were careful. They always added that there was a 'meeting' at such and such a place. So the important meetings and late nights that Michael was busy with? More like he was busy with LeAnn."

Chase ran his hands down his face. What an ass. Michael had had everything and he'd ruined it. He ruined Julia's memory of him and their family. He was mad as hell for her.

"I called her."

He dropped his hands and tried not to let his mouth hang

open. She had guts. If there was one thing he knew about this woman, it was that she had guts, and a heart of gold and it'd been broken way too many times.

"She admitted everything. She was married too."

He cursed under his breath. "I'm sorry as hell. I never knew. And I would never think Mike would do that. Not to you...to Matthew. He always spoke of you like you were his entire world." He realized his words actually hurt her, because who the hell wanted to hear that?

"It took me a long time to process. At first I thought I was being paranoid as I read those emails and then I knew that I was in serious denial if I thought it wasn't true. That's why I had to call her. I had to know."

"I'm sorry, Julia. I, uh, hell, I had no idea."

"I believe you," she said. She placed her hands in her pockets and for a moment she looked sad, vulnerable. He had seen her on her most vulnerable days, her saddest days. That she had let him in at that time, had been an honor to him. What he'd seen of her, even broken, was that Julia had guts. She was a fighter. She was a woman who loved deeply, but she was a woman who kept going.

"Me too. I think I'm most sorry because he ruined my memory of my perfect little family. He left me with unanswered questions. I will never know why. I will never be able to yell at him and demand those answers. For a long time I blamed myself. Had I let myself go after Matthew, was that why? Was he jealous of the time I spent between work and our son?"

He had to stifle his choice words and his need to rip apart his best friend. But he couldn't stand here and watch her blame herself. "No," he said, the word coming out harshly. "It wasn't you. It was all on him. You both took vows. As a husband, as a father, he owed you honesty. Here's the thing. You want out of a marriage? You get out. Then you move on, not before. He owed you that. At the very least, he owed you the dignity of being honest with you."

She blinked back tears and it took all his self-control not to wrap her up in his arms. But it didn't seem right now, everything darkened by what she'd revealed. "I just…Michael was everything I ever thought I wanted in a man. He was smart and caring and responsible…" Her voice trailed off and she was looking faraway and he ignored the bitter sting of jealousy as he listened to her speak of another man—his best friend. "But then after I found out I started analyzing our relationship. Was it everything I ever thought? Or was I naive? I mean, I never…" Her eyes darted away from him, but not before he caught a glimmer of embarrassment. "I didn't even have a boyfriend before Michael. What did I know about guys? What did I know about anything?"

He ran his hand over his jaw, hating that she doubted herself. "You're smart and you're loving and you're honest. So right there, you're a helluva lot better than a lot of people. As for Michael? I didn't see that coming and he was my best friend years before you met him. And what about me? I was with plenty of women before I got married…" He coughed when she gave him a pointed look. "And I never saw Sandy walking out on us. Never. Yeah, in retrospect I probably should have detected something, but who the hell could predict that?"

"Didn't it make you want to never let anyone close again?"

Anyone except Julia. "I'd make an exception for the right woman."

She looked down at her boots. "You know, Chase, when I was in the city, I didn't really get to know anyone. I didn't want to know anyone. Sure, I was familiar with my colleagues, there were men…who asked me out, but I wasn't interested in anyone. It's like I doubted that there were any really good men left in the world, because I thought I'd been married to one of the good guys and that shattered me."

He understood exactly. "There are days when I wonder if there are any decent people out there anymore. There are days when all I see are the rotten scum in the world and I worry for Maggie, I worry what kind of a world will this be for her one day? For her kids? And then I'll come upon an accident, and there'll be strangers there, with their cars stopped, draping blankets around the people in the accident, calling in 911, helping complete strangers until the paramedics and cops show up. There are good people still around. Sometimes, at different points in our lives, I think we have to search harder, but they're there." His voice had turned hoarse at the sight of the tears in her eyes. Tears in Julia's eyes always gutted him. She gave a little sniffle.

"When did you become so…"

"Sappy?"

She laughed and he smiled at the sound of it, at the ability he had to make her laugh. She nodded and then shook her head, her smile dipping slightly. "Sweet?"

"Don't tell anyone."

"I think people around here must know it."

"I think Maggie is responsible. She brings out a different side. I have to be a better man, for her."

She didn't say anything for a second, but her eyes were filled with something. "Chase," she whispered.

"Tell me."

"I miss him," she said, so softly he almost didn't hear. "I miss my baby so much. I don't talk about him. I know people say it gets easier and you should talk about the people who you loved and are now gone, but I can't, and I think it's a lie. At least for me. I can't talk about my baby and be happy. I remember him every second of every day because he is in my soul, he *is* my soul. But I can't talk about him…easily, because

I'll get caught up in a funny memory and it'll be okay for the moment. It will fill me so completely with love and then in a second it's gone, when I remember the little boy I'm talking about is dead, and that…that feeling, that emptiness is so bad, that I just…cave and go dark inside. I'm not strong enough to talk about him."

He blinked away the moisture in his eyes and stared at the woman claiming not to be strong; the strongest woman he'd ever known. And God how he wished he could make everything right for her, that he could be a man good enough for her. But he'd never made promises he couldn't keep and he never lied. Maybe that's not what she needed. Maybe she just needed him right now, the way he was, because for some reason the way she looked at him…he walked that last step into her and pulled her against him. Julia melted into him, her soft curves pressed against his body. It wasn't the first time he noticed how they fit together. No one had ever fit him like Julia. Her arms wrapped around his waist and he felt her deep breath against him.

He brushed his lips against her head, inhaling the sweet smell of the woman he wanted desperately. "You'll be happy again, Julia. I promise you."

Neither of them said anything for a few moments, and he just held her until it sounded like an earthquake was starting. Sure enough his daughter came barrelling down the road, with Gwen chasing after her. "Daddy!"

He stifled his groan and backed up a step, the mood broken once again. There was one thing he was fairly certain of—whatever this attraction was he had to Julia, she felt it too. There would be no walking away this time without really knowing what they'd be like together. This would be the Christmas to show her just how good they'd be together.

Chapter Nine

She needed to survive Christmas.

Julia knew the chances of her leaving Shadow Creek unscathed after Christmas were becoming slimmer and slimmer. Chase and his daughter were roping her in. Maggie had called her this morning, begging her to come and find a Christmas tree with them. Somehow she'd convinced her father to set up a tree at their current home and then another when they moved. The day had been fun and there was something different in the air between her and Chase.

She couldn't deny, as silly as it sounded, that seeing Chase cut down the large tree, haul it onto his truck, and bring it home for his little girl was...undeniably attractive. He was undeniably hot. And when was the last time she'd thought of a man like that? Even Michael had never evoked this kind of...passion in her. In other words, she'd never wanted to jump his bones. As she stood there, watching him position the tree in the stand, muscles rippling, perfectly efficient, strong, capable, that's exactly what she felt like doing.

After last night, knowing that he knew nothing about

Michael's affair, she felt a weight lift from her shoulders, and the memory of standing on the street, in his arms, played over and over in her mind as she slept.

She cleared her throat. "You know what? Why don't I make us some hot chocolate while we wait for Daddy to get that set up?"

"Yay!" yelled Maggie.

"Great. As soon as I finish this, I'll haul the decorations in from the garage," Chase said, without taking his head out of the underside of the tree. She practically ran out of the room when she realized she was checking him out, taking in the long legs in those jeans, the washboard abs that she'd catch glimpses of when his shirt rode up. She was a disaster.

Minutes later she was stirring some dark cocoa into the pot of milk. Maggie was sitting at the breakfast bar, spreading out all the candies that she was planning on decorating her gingerbread house with. "I've never made a gingerbread house before," she said with a big grin.

"I used to make them every Christmas with my mom. My favorite part was sneaking candies while I was decorating the house," she said, remembering her childhood fondly. She refused to let the pain of her bittersweet memory of her own son, and the fact that she had never been able to continue that tradition with him, overwhelm her. And she refused to wonder where she'd be next year, how she could go back to her condo in the city, knowing that Maggie and Chase were here.

"I need hot chocolate, now," Chase said with a grin, walking into the kitchen.

Julia gave him a salute. "Right away, Sheriff." She walked over to the stove to pour.

"Julia, we both know you're not the type of woman to take orders," he whispered, his deep voice filled with humor and something else. The something else that was currently making her blood hotter than the liquid in the pot. He was standing behind her, the heat from his body warming her. He had spoken almost in her ear and she knew if she tilted back slightly she'd feel him behind her.

"I'm not sure if that was a compliment or a complaint," she answered, cringing at the breathlessness in her voice.

"Always a compliment, always," he said, reaching around her to pour the hot chocolate into the waiting snowman mugs. He smelled of the crisp outdoors and pine and she wanted nothing more than to turn around, face him and kiss him, regardless of what would happen. Instead, she stood there, forcing herself to look normal, sound normal.

"Daddy, did you get the decorations? We have to stay on schedule. First the tree, then I'm doing the gingerbread house. Don't forget the hot chocolate."

"My work is never done," he said under his breath, grabbing a cup, his warm fingers brushing against hers. She was glad when she heard them walking to the tree so she could compose herself for a moment. She took a deep breath and then another, before turning. Father and daughter were standing in front of the tree that now stood proudly in the great room, admiring it. Julia admired them.

"Auntie Julia, you make the best hot chocolate!" Maggie said, placing her cup down on the end table.

Julia took a sip of the warm chocolate drink and walked over to join them. "I'm glad you like it, honey."

"I think it's the best I've ever had too," Chase said.

Once they finished their drinks, they started rummaging through the boxes and spent the next hour or so decorating the tree and stringing the lights. By the time they'd finished, dusk was setting in and the snow had picked up, and along with it a howling wind.

"Looks like that storm they were warning us about is starting," Chase said. Julia caught the worry in his voice as he looked out the window.

"I was hoping maybe the weather reports were wrong."

"Never wrong when it's bad weather."

"Okay, now that we're done with this, it's time to move on to the gingerbread house!" Maggie obviously wasn't concerned with the weather in the least.

Chase laughed. "Aren't you tired? Maybe we should save that for tomorrow. Why don't we order some takeout or something?"

"Daddy."

"If it's still okay with you, Chase, I don't mind making the house with Maggie. I haven't made one of these in years," she said. Maggie ran over to her and almost toppled them both over as she hugged Julia.

The look in Chase's eyes made her heart squeeze. "If it's okay with you, then it's okay with me."

"This is the best day of my life!" Maggie squealed as she ran out of the room.

Chase and Julia stood there looking at each other. The wind howled and the only other sound was Maggie unwrapping packages of candy in the kitchen. "Thanks for making this day so special for Maggie…for both of us."

Julia blinked back tears. He adored his little girl, and she saw this softer side of him whenever she was around. "Thanks for including me."

They didn't move and she wondered when this had become so awkward. She also wondered what he'd do if it were just the two of them in here. She knew he felt what she was feeling. It was becoming impossible to ignore. She wondered if he'd walk across the room and kiss her. She also knew that thinking about him kissing her was not a wise thing to do because she was now having difficulty maintaining eye contact with the man.

Julia tilted her head toward the door. "I should probably

go help her before she eats the candy and there's none left for the actual house."

. . .

"Ah hell," Chase muttered, an hour later as he looked at his phone. "I'm sorry, ladies, but I gotta leave. We've got to close down the main roads heading into the county and there's a pileup at least six cars out." He was gathering his gear as he spoke, mentally running down what needed to get done before he got out there. "I'll call Cassy and see if you can stay there tonight, Maggie."

"I'll stay. Here. With Maggie."

He couldn't say anything over the sound of Maggie screeching with glee and dancing around. "Julia, are you sure? I don't know when I'm going to get back," he said, shrugging into his winter jacket. It was going to be brutal out there tonight. He studied her face, noticing she looked pale.

She placed her arms around Maggie and gave her a hug. "Of course I'm sure. I'll stay, don't give us a second thought."

"I'm going to get out our Christmas DVDs," Maggie said, running out of the room.

Julia followed him to the front door and he shoved his boots on while she stood by quietly. Something was off. "You don't have to stay, you know. She has a backpack that's always ready to go in case I get called into work and I can easily drop her off."

"Chase. Stop. I'm more than happy to spend the night with Maggie."

He stood and zipped up his jacket, looking at her. His radio was going off non-stop now and he lowered it. One minute wouldn't change the world.

"Bye, Maggie," he called out. She ran to the front door, gave him a kiss and then ran out. He laughed. "I think you made her night."

Julia gave him a small smile. "Chase?"

His hand was on the doorknob, his mind slowly leaving the house and onto whatever was waiting for him out there tonight.

Suddenly, she was reaching up to him, her arms wrapping around him. "Please be careful," she whispered and he could have sworn he heard tears in her voice, felt a tremor run through her. Jesus. It was him, she was worried about him. He pulled back, bending at the knees slightly to look into her gorgeous green eyes. "I always am. I have a lot to come home to," he said, his own voice gruff.

She nodded repeatedly, but the worry didn't go away.

"I always come back, Julia," he said, this time more forcefully.

Then he stepped out into the blizzard and it hit him, the night of Michael and Matthew's accident. Of course she looked ill. This was bringing back all sorts of horrible memories, and maybe that's what it had to do with, certainly more of that, and less of worry for him.

He pulled his SUV out of the driveway, wipers at full speed, forcing his mind off his irrational hurt and stupid sappiness, and trying to focus on the road, when there was zero visibility.

• • •

Julia forced herself to smile, to focus on having a fun night with Maggie, despite being anxious and panicky. "So what do you want to do first?" Maggie asked.

She tapped her chin and looked around the kitchen. "How about I get some dinner started for us?"

"Sure! Can I help?"

"Of course you can. What do you feel like eating?" She

opened the fridge and frowned slightly, trying to figure out what she could make with the items in there. Their options were looking very limited.

"Hmm. Spaghetti and meatballs?"

Julia grimaced. "I don't know if we have the right stuff for that, sweetie."

"Oh. Yeah. Daddy doesn't really cook. He tries to, but he says his talents are limited to bacon and eggs. So that's what he makes me on Saturdays and he always makes them into a smiley face for me," she said with a grin.

Oh, how her heart was in this constant state of squeezing whenever she was around this child.

Maggie continued, "Usually on Sundays we go to Auntie Cassy's and Uncle Edward's house, and they give us leftovers so Daddy doesn't have to cook on Monday. Tuesday and Wednesday nights I eat dinner there and stay there after school until Daddy is finished at work. Thursday is Mrs. Peter's day and she cleans up and does laundry and stuff and always starts dinner. Usually it's beef stew and biscuits and it's really good. And then Friday, Daddy and I get pizza. That's my favorite."

Julia knew how hard Chase worked, but when Maggie spelled out the days of the week, the full impact of all that he was juggling by himself hit her. He adored Maggie and it was obvious he was doing everything to make her childhood as good as he could, but she knew his job was demanding and yet somehow he made his little girl feel loved and safe and cherished. "Your daddy is a hard-working guy, isn't he?"

Maggie nodded vigorously. "He is, Auntie Julia. He says we're two peas in a pod. Something about me being even more stubborn than him!"

Julia laughed.

"On Saturday mornings he tries to sleep in," she said with a giggle.

"Uh oh, but you don't let him?"

She shook her head, giggling. "I'm so happy it's Saturday and I can't wait to see him," she said. "So I jump into his bed and he grumbles and puts the pillow over his head," she said, making exaggerated moaning noises and arm gestures. "And then I ask him if I can watch shows in his bed while he sleeps."

"What does he say?" Julia asked, already knowing the answer.

"He mumbles so I grab the remote and put on the Disney channel and get under the covers and then Daddy always reaches out to hold my hand even though he's sleeping. Once, when he was super tired, he said he'd pay me five dollars if I could stop talking for five minutes," she said with a giggle. "I told him bribery was illegal."

Julia burst out laughing. "Oh, Maggie, you're the best," she said.

Maggie beamed. "I think you're the best, too. And you make my dad so happy. Look, there's your picture."

Julia's throat constricted as she saw the old picture of herself. It had been taken on Matthew's second birthday. She had looked so young. So happy. It was like she was staring at a different person. She didn't recognize that person anymore.

"Well, your dad is a special guy. You know, why don't we make him some yummy food and maybe some dessert, too? I bet he'll be really hungry when he gets home."

Maggie jumped up and down. "I think there's more food in the freezer. Mrs. Peter does groceries and she's always saying that the house needs to be stocked with staples, whatever that means."

Julia rummaged through the freezer, finding some ground beef. That was a start. She rolled up her sleeves and looked around. There was a basket of Maggie's laundry that needed folding. Dinner needed to be made. Judging by what was in the pantry, she might even be able to make some cookies with

Maggie.

"Okay, Maggie. How about you and I make some dinner, do some clean up, and then bake cookies?"

"Yes! I'll be the best helper you ever had," she said, running up and wrapping her arms around Julia's waist. Julia kissed the top of her head and then started delegating.

Three hours later, the winds and snow outside had increased drastically and it took all of her self-discipline to not let her worry for Chase show, but every time ice pellets would tap against the window she jumped a little. The image of him trudging through the snow to his truck, all tough, tall, and fearless played over and over again. Chase was tough as nails, and he meant so much more to her than a dear friend. Maybe that was part of her fear; she was finally opening up again, maybe in a way that she never ever had.

But she hadn't told him. She had been so busy running and guarding herself, she hadn't even hinted at her feelings for him, and now...he was out in this blizzard, helping other people, putting his own life on the line and she hadn't even told him...what he meant to her. Life couldn't be so cruel to take him too.

She forced herself to calm down as she heard Maggie's footsteps approaching. The kitchen was clean and tidy, Maggie's laundry neatly folded. They had cooked and eaten together. She had the sauce on low, ready for when Chase came home, whenever that would be.

"Can I have another sugar cookie, Auntie Julia?" Maggie was standing in the doorway, wearing candy cane flannel pajamas and looking so cute, she had to smile despite her worry.

"I think I'm going to get in trouble for letting you have four. Besides, you can have more tomorrow and I'm sure your daddy is going to eat a bunch when he gets home tonight."

Maggie nodded agreeably. "He loves cookies and I don't

mind sharing."

"Good girl. All ready for bed?"

"Yup. Brushed my teeth really well too. Can you tuck me in?"

"Of course I can," she said as they walked out of the kitchen. Julia turned on the table lamp on Maggie's nightstand and plumped her pillow and turned down the covers.

"I love your room, Maggie."

Maggie beamed as she settled under the covers. "Me too. Daddy and I worked on it together when I started first grade. I told him I couldn't really have a baby room anymore because grade one is a big deal, you know?"

Julia stifled her grin as she sat next to Maggie. "I agree. Grade one is a big deal."

"I got to pick out the paint color and Daddy painted and I was his assistant."

"You make a good team."

Maggie's smile faltered slightly. "We have to be. It's just me and him. Sometimes I worry he won't come back and when I was little, I worried about it a lot."

Julia smoothed Maggie's dark hair from her forehead while she tried to find her voice. But Maggie beat her to it. "Sometimes I'd have nightmares that he left with my mom, but then Daddy always came back, and whenever I'd have a nightmare he'd let me sleep in his bed and I knew nothing else bad would happen. And he said to me that there was nothing in the world that would keep him from getting home to me. So now I never worry," she said.

Julia stared at Chase's little girl and fought the emotion that was swirling through her uncontrollably. She was so much like her father. She was so sure, and she believed in Chase. She quickly swiped at a tear that escaped.

She would never tell Maggie that her dad couldn't really promise something like that, but she believed it, and Julia desperately wanted to believe it. She wanted to be able to sit in this room and enjoy being with his little girl, without fearing for his life. She wished the sound of the wind howling and the ice pellets hitting the window didn't make her stomach churn with dread, but they did. She was falling in love with Chase and she didn't know what to do about it. Chase's life was in danger every day. Being with a man like him, loving a man like him, meant opening herself up to loss all over again. She wouldn't feel calm until Chase walked through that door, whatever time it was.

"I'm sorry, Auntie Julia," Maggie whispered, looking worried now.

Julia shook her head. "Why are you sorry? I'm being silly, that's all."

"My dad told me about your little boy and your husband. I think what I said reminded you of them." Her lower lip trembled as she stared at Julia. Julia took a ragged breath and squeezed Maggie's hand.

"You didn't say anything wrong. Expressing your feelings is never wrong and you don't have to be afraid of mentioning Matthew and Michael. I think about my little boy all the time, honey. He's right here," she whispered, touching her heart. "It's impossible for me to forget him. Don't ever be afraid of talking to me, okay?"

Maggie gave her a shaky smile. "Then can I ask you something about being a mom?"

Julia nodded.

"Because I asked my dad, but sometimes I think it's hard for him, and he's not a mom, so I don't know if his answers are really right. Did your little boy do anything really bad? Like so bad that you wanted to leave him?"

Oh God. She didn't breathe for a moment, knowing Maggie was watching her closely. "Honey, there is nothing my baby could have done to make me leave him. What happened with your mom was her fault. It was something in her that made her need to leave, it had nothing to do with you. You're the sweetest, most precious little girl I've ever met," she said with a smile, trying to find humor in an impossible situation.

"My daddy is so special, Julia."

Julia sucked in a breath.

"She shouldn't have left him too."

Julia leaned down to kiss Maggie's forehead. "You're very smart, Maggie. Just as smart as him, and you're right. Your daddy is special. The best."

Maggie's features relaxed and she turned slightly under the covers, her eyelids looking heavy now. "It's really past my bedtime, isn't it?"

"Way past," Julia said, leaning down to kiss her soft cheek. "You have a good night's sleep, okay, sweetheart? I'll be downstairs."

Maggie nodded and Julia turned off her lamp.

"Auntie Julia?" Maggie called out when she was almost out the door.

Julia paused. "Yes?"

"I'm glad you and my dad are good friends."

"Me too, sweetie."

"I'm glad you make him so happy. And when he's happy, I'm happy. I know that grownups have girlfriends and boyfriends and get married and stuff, but my dad doesn't. He's all by himself and that makes me sad for him. But now that you're here, he doesn't seem alone anymore."

Julia clutched the door frame and a flood of feeling stole through her. "I'm glad," she said, stupidly, unable to come up with anything else to say, but it didn't seem to matter because Maggie's eyes were shut. She stood there, looking at Chase's daughter, feeling all those feelings she used to have for her little boy. The love, the maternal instincts to protect and cherish and love. They flooded her until she almost couldn't stand.

She stood there, drowning in emotion she hadn't felt for another child since Matthew was taken from her. The most shocking part was that she didn't want it gone, she didn't want to hide it. Maggie was slowly making her whole again, a new version of the woman she once was, living a different life than she had before.

Because of Maggie.

And Chase.

Chapter Ten

Chase had been bone tired many times. Ass-frozen, bone-cold, bone-tired was different. The general feeling that people were idiots for not adjusting speed and driving based on road conditions had been the consensus tonight. If he could have handed out tickets based solely on stupidity alone he would have, gladly. It was a miracle, really, that there hadn't been any serious injuries tonight.

He backed his SUV into the driveway, not expecting to see any lights on but the porch lights were, and he could see the front hall lamp was too. It was typical of Julia to think of someone else. She and Maggie must have fallen asleep hours ago. Right now, he didn't even care that his stomach was growling. All he wanted was to fall into a deep sleep and wake up at least eight hours later. He hauled his ass out of the car, not even flinching when the snow and ice mix pelted his face; he was immune at this point. He trudged up the front steps and stopped short as the front door whipped open and Julia stood there, the expression on her face one no one had ever given him. And then she flew down the steps and he caught her in his arms, immediately walking into the house, and shutting the door behind him. He leaned against it, holding her to him as emotion assaulted his tired body.

"Thank God you're okay," she whispered against his neck. His arms tightened around her and he didn't think he'd ever let her go. She had stayed up for him. He pulled his head back to look at her, and every single emotion he'd ever wanted to see from her was staring back at him in her green eyes. He clenched his jaw, and reached out to tangle his hands in her hair, just like he'd dreamed of doing at least a thousand times. But he didn't look away from her eyes, needing to know that she accepted this, that she wanted him.

"I was so worried about you," she whispered again, her fingers grasping the hair at the nape of his neck and tugging him to her.

She wanted him. It was there, in the way she reached up for him, the way her eyes went from his eyes to his lips. He leaned down and kissed her, finally tasting the lips of the woman he'd wanted his entire goddamn adult life. She opened her mouth beneath his, and all thoughts of being tired vanished. He devoured her, unable to think of anything except the woman in his arms. She pressed close to him and he felt every soft curve mold to him. His hands went from her hair to her body, slowly, greedily, wanting to feel her, to memorize in case this one night was all they had.

She let out the sexiest moan against his lips as his hands grazed the sides of her breasts. He cursed softly, wanting to take things slow, not wanting to scare her off, but completely unable to slow down. He picked her up until she straddled his waist.

"Maggie sleeping?" he managed to whisper against her mouth.

She nodded, her hands grasping at the collar of his jacket and helping him shrug out of it. It landed on the ground with a thud, and he walked up the stairs, not letting her go, not stopping until they reached his bed. He released her and then strode across the room to shut and lock his door. Then he was back, covering Julia with his body. She met him halfway.

"I've wanted you, Jules, for so long," he whispered as he trailed kisses down her neck, his hands working to get her out of her sweater.

She paused for a moment when her sweater came off. He took in the gorgeous sight in front of him, the pale blue lace bra, and her luscious breasts spilling over the rim. She gave him a look he didn't fully get before taking off his shirt. A shiver stole through her and then her hands were tracing his shoulders, down his biceps.

The vulnerability stamped across her features made him pause for a moment. And then he kissed her, expressing with his mouth, his hands, his body that this meant so much more to him than just one night. Julia had returned to him for Christmas, she was in his home, in his bed, and he was going to spend the rest of the night showing her what he always knew—that they were meant for each other. He would show her how cherished he could make her.

Chase made the turn at the highest speed he could, given the heavy rain. Sweat had dampened his shirt, making it uncomfortable under his uniform coat. It was November. Nighttime. The call that had come in about the car collision had made every hair stand at attention on the back of his neck, and then his gut had churned. He'd made a U-turn and headed out to the reported scene, probably beating the paramedics.

He eased his foot off the gas, but hadn't been able to loosen his tightly clenched hands on the steering wheel. He squinted as smoke and headlights appeared in the distance. The wipers were going at full speed and it was still almost impossible to see. As he approached, he saw there was already another squad car on scene, lights flashing, the roads already closed in either direction. He hopped out of the car, running, his need to get to the car that barely even resembled a car propelling him forward, faster. He needed to get there, inside, even though he knew there were no survivors the way that car was wrapped around the tree. He knew that car.

"Hands off!" he yelled to the young cop that tried to tell him not to bother. He reached in, the bodies a mangled mess, not recognizable to the eye, but to the gut. God, no, there was no way he'd let Michael and Matthew go like this. "I'm getting you out," he heard himself yell, cry, to people who couldn't hear him anymore. "Dammit, Michael, I'm getting your boy out of here." He didn't know if it was the rain, or if it was his tears, but he could barely see as he reached inside the car.

"Lieutenant, get over here," he yelled.

"I'm searching for the other car. There was another car, tracks down the mountain."

He needed to go. He needed to go and help the survivors. He knew what he'd been trained to do…but now, shit…Julia was here.

"Julia, hold on…" But her head was dangling loosely, unnaturally. She was covered in blood, just like the rest of them. "Don't you dare die, I've got you, I promise."

The rain started again. He was sweating and swearing and he needed to get to her.

"Chase, Chase, wake up."

It was her. It was Julia. But she was dead.

Hands gripped his arms, shaking him.

His eyes sprung open. Julia. She was shaking him, beside him, in his bed. Naked. Alive.

"You terrified me. Are you okay?" She was smoothing

hair off his forehead. He swiped the moisture from his eyes and face, and focused on her, and on taking deep breaths. The dream wasn't new. It was a recurring nightmare from the night he'd found Michael and Matthew. It had tormented him. Some nights early on it made him throw up. The nightmares were less frequent now. But Julia—she had never been in the dream.

He stared at her gorgeous face, eyes serious, brow furrowed as she stared at him. "What happened, what was it?"

He shook his head, knowing he was going to lie. He would do anything for this woman. He would tell her anything, give her anything, but he couldn't give her the truth about this. She'd been through hell; she didn't need to know this. They had never spoken about what he'd seen that night and he was fine bearing the brunt of that.

He raised his hand, hating that it was still shaking. "Just a stupid nightmare. I'm okay."

She grasped his hand in hers, squeezing it.

He closed his eyes for a moment, forcing the image of her lying there in the car out of his mind. He opened his eyes, raising his other hand, scrunching fistfuls of her hair, gently pulling her forward, on top of him. He knew he'd wanted her forever. He knew he loved her, but not like this. Her mouth hovered close to his and he knew she was the only one who could erase all of it tonight.

• • •

Julia opened her eyes and glanced at the display on the clock. It was a different clock because she was at Chase's house, in his bed. The sleep washed away and memories of last night lapped in gently. She felt warm, safe, happy.

Chase's deep, steady breathing at her neck, his strong arm around her waist, made it very clear to her groggy mind why she felt this way—him. A wave of memories washed over her; she had never experienced anything like what they'd shared last night. It had nothing to do with experience, or talent on his part, it had been real, raw, and a passion that she didn't know she possessed had consumed her. She had never felt so wanted, and she had never wanted someone as much. Chase kissed her and touched her like no one ever had. He kissed her with a gentle possession, an all-consuming desire. He captured a part of her that she didn't know existed. She and Michael had been…more friends than anything, she realized now. Maybe that was it…maybe he'd found this kind of passion with someone else.

This was going to change everything. She couldn't deny her feelings for him anymore, but what did that mean for them? The things he'd whispered to her. She shut her eyes as she remembered the sound of his voice, the scrape of his stubble against her skin, and shivered. How would she ever be able to leave him? And if she stayed, how would she ever be able to surrender her worry?

She stopped breathing when she thought she heard noise in the hall. *Maggie.* She rose from bed, careful not to disturb Chase and quietly and quickly dressed in the dark room. She didn't want Maggie to find her in here and confuse the little girl. She tiptoed out of the room, pausing for a moment to look back at the man sleeping so soundly in the bed.

Heat flashed through her body. She would never be able to look at him the same way again, knowing this other side of him. He was beautiful. Rugged and strong, gentle and tender. Noise again in the hallway reminded her she was on her way out of the room, not staying.

A glance down the hallway confirmed that Maggie was awake, because the bathroom light was on. She quickly went to the spare room and gathered the toothbrush that Chase had given her and turned on the light. Sure enough, a few seconds later, Maggie was knocking quietly on the door.

She opened it and her heart swelled at the sight of Maggie's excited smile.

"I'm so happy you're still here!"

Julia ruffled the top of Maggie's head. "Me too, sweetie. I'm going to clean up a bit in the washroom and then I'll meet you downstairs, okay? Let's be quiet so that your daddy can sleep. He got home really late last night."

Maggie nodded sagely. "Okay, I'll tiptoe," she said in a theatrical whisper that didn't really sound that much softer than her normal voice. Her exaggerated tiptoe was quiet however, and it did bring a smile to Julia's face as she watched her walk down the hallway.

Half an hour later, Maggie was happily eating the first batch of pancakes they had made together while Julia sipped coffee and turned bacon in the frying pan.

"Daddy is going to be so excited when he wakes up and sees all this breakfast! It's his favorite meal of the day. He even makes it for dinner!"

Julia smiled at Maggie. "Well, this will be a nice surprise for him then, and I bet he's going to be super hungry because he was working so late."

"How did you know?" Coffee sloshed over the rim of her mug at the sound of Chase's deep voice. He walked into the kitchen and gave Maggie a kiss on the head before walking over to her.

"You made all this for me?"

She shrugged, smiling, as she watched him take the lid off the pot and inhale. He was walking around the kitchen, shrugging into a T-shirt, and a pair of low-slung jeans. Chase was…beautiful. He was a beautiful person on the inside and out. And good God, did the man know what he was doing in bed. He poured himself a cup of coffee and then opened the fridge, his eyes widening.

"Oh, that was last night's dinner. It's easy to reheat," she said.

He turned to her. "You cooked?"

"Baked too! Soooooo many cookies, Daddy! We can eat them all!"

They all laughed as they sat down at the table together. "Thank you. You didn't have to do that. I owe you one." The way he said that, with a glint in his eye, and the corner of his mouth turned up made her face turn red.

"Uh, that's fine."

"No, I insist."

"Maybe later tonight?"

She opened her mouth but the grin he gave her was contagious. "We'll see, Sheriff. I'll review your offer as the day goes on."

He laughed, low and throaty, and her lower belly stirred. She quickly drank her coffee and avoided eye contact with him.

"So I was thinking of taking Maggie over to the new place tomorrow once we get the keys. Do you have time to come by?"

"Say yes, Julia!" Maggie said, maple syrup dripping down her face.

"How can I say no to that face?" Julia laughed, leaning across and wiping the adorable little girl's face.

Seriously. How was she supposed to say no to either of them?

Chapter Eleven

"Julia, is that you?"

Julia stepped into her in-laws' kitchen later that evening. They knew she'd spent the night at Chase and Maggie's—babysitting, which was true, and anything beyond that she wasn't ready to share yet.

She felt like a new woman, or maybe she felt like the woman she was always supposed to be. Everything about last night had been right. When she had panicked and had been sucked into the vortex of the memory of her worst night, something had come over her. It had been the realization that holding back and shielding herself from hurt wasn't the way she wanted to live. When Chase's SUV had pulled into the driveway and she had that first glimpse of him, all her reservations and fears had vanished and were replaced with only the need to hold on to him. Everything that had happened after that…she knew in her heart she loved Chase and Maggie and no matter what, she wouldn't be able to deny that. Now she just needed to figure out what she was going to do about it.

"It is," she called out as she entered the kitchen.

Cassy was seated at the kitchen table wrapping presents. Rolls of brightly colored, shiny paper and ribbons and bows were piled at one end of the table, while Cassy was at the other with tape, scissors and a box about to get wrapped. A bright red candle glowed from a simple glass hurricane and Nat King Cole's voice soothingly filled the room. It wasn't the first time she'd seen this setting; a few years ago she, Gwen, Cassy, and her mother had wrapped gifts together while drinking eggnog and sharing many laughs.

"Is it just you tonight?" She settled in at the table beside Cassy, motioning for a box to wrap.

Cassy nodded and passed the tape. "Yes, and I'm enjoying it. I hadn't started any gift wrapping and usually I'm all finished by the first. Edward and Gwen are at the shop; he's helping them with a few things. I have to do the wrapping when Edward is out of the house. He's just like a child, always trying to find out what I've bought him."

Julia smiled. "Well, you're doing better than I am. I haven't even started my shopping! I wanted to do all of it in Shadow Creek thinking I'd have loads of time. I'll have to set aside time tomorrow for sure."

"Don't you worry, I'm sure you'll be able to get it done quite quickly. The downtown is small but has everything a person needs. Ambiance, charm, and the essentials."

Julia smiled as she positioned a red bow in the middle of the box she'd finished wrapping. Cassy was always putting in a plug for Shadow Creek every chance she got. "You're right about that. That's why I saved my shopping for here."

"Well, perfect. I'm sure you've been so busy between the commercial rental and…Chase and Maggie," she said, giving her a sidelong glance.

She slid the wrapped gift across the table to Cassy so she could fill out the gift tag and then moved onto another one.

She needed to keep a straight face. "Yes, it's been busy," she said, in what she hoped was a nonchalant voice.

"That was some storm last night. I always worry about Chase when he's out there in that kind of weather," Cassy said, shaking her head and starting on another gift.

Julia stopped wrapping for a moment and Cassy met her stare, both of them lost for a moment and she knew where they both were—right back to the night of the accident that robbed them both so savagely. Julia tried to blink back the moisture that had suddenly flooded her vision. "I was so scared, Cassy."

Cassy nodded. "I know, darling. I know. I always pray when he goes out there. Chase is like a son to me, and little Maggie like a granddaughter. He's tough, and like he says, he always comes back."

Julia managed a smile. "He does like to say that." She remembered exactly how he looked, standing there, when he'd said that.

"Well, he believes it and I choose to believe it too. We have to let go of fear, I learned, or it will kill us and stop us from living."

Julia nodded, forcing herself to wrap the next gift.

"He's quite the man. You know most wouldn't be capable of handling everything like he does. I mean, a demanding and consuming career, raising a little girl, and juggling everything. But he does it so well and makes it look easy."

She avoided Cassy's intense gaze and didn't answer right away. The sound of scissors and tape and music kept them company as she contemplated her answer. "You're right. He makes it all look so easy."

Cassy didn't miss a beat. "Yes. It's awful what Sandy did to the both of them. He was devastated. I think mostly for Maggie's sake. It's not as though he and Sandy had a great love, but it was a betrayal of the worst kind and he didn't even have a chance to properly grieve. He had to keep it all together and be a father to his little girl."

He had been betrayed, and so had she, but she could never tell that to Cassy. It wouldn't be fair. Michael had been a good son to them; she would take this secret to the grave. There was no way they knew.

"Don't you think?" Cassy said after a moment.

She looked up from the gift she'd finished wrapping. "I agree. He's been through so much."

Cassy nodded, satisfied with her answer. "And so have you."

She quickly stood. This conversation was getting too heavy and Cassy wasn't letting anything drop. "I think I'll make a cup of tea. Would you like one?"

Cassy winked at her. "I'd love one, dear. I have a gingerbread spiced tea in the cupboard beside the stove."

She busied herself with filling up the kettle and hoping that Cassy would drop the subject. She found the teabags and dropped them in the snowman mugs and waited for the water to boil. So far Cassy had busied herself with another gift while she hummed along to the radio.

She handed Cassy her cup a few minutes later and sat down across from her, picking out another boxed gift and then selecting some candy cane printed wrapping paper. Steam and the aroma of gingerbread filled the air as they worked in silence for a few moments. "Maybe Gwen will have time to go shopping tomorrow," she said. They needed to start their morning walks.

"Mm-hmm. I know for a fact Chase does a lot of his shopping at Harrison's Menswear," she said before taking a sip of tea. She stared at Julia over the rim of the snowman cup. Cassy didn't miss a beat.

"Thanks. I'll keep that in mind."

"I imagine he'd be a large in most clothing items, being so tall and fit with those broad shoulders."

Julia threw a bow at her, unable to hold in her laughter anymore. Cassy put on an innocent face and tried not to laugh. "What is it, dear? Don't you agree?"

She was not about to discuss Chase's hot body with her mother-in-law. Or the fact that she'd seen said hot body without clothes and it was even better than she had imagined. "Cassy."

"I believe in being honest and open about these things. You know you're like a daughter to me, Julia, and I want you to be happy."

Julia stared across the table at her, the mood shifting faster than the high winds outside. The slight sting of tears caught the back of her eyes. Her mother-in-law was a force to be reckoned with. She was so strong. "I know, and I feel the same way about you and Edward. You are my second parents. I just…I haven't been able to fully move on."

"I know you haven't, but it's time, dear. Five years is a long time for a young woman to be alone. How can you ever truly heal if you don't allow yourself to love again?"

Her throat constricted painfully. "I don't know how you do it, Cassy. You're so strong. You lost your son and your grandson. Jack left town, I left because neither of us could deal. But you stayed. You stayed and continued living your life."

Cassy put down her mug and leaned across the table and gripped Julia's hand. Her chin was set, her eyes lit with a ferocity she'd witnessed from her on occasion. "I have faith, a deep, unwavering faith that somehow everything will be okay. I never lost it. On my worst days I never lost it. It's what I wake to in the morning, and it's what I fall asleep to at night. It has been tried and it was tested that day when I had to watch my babies lowered into the ground. Then when Jack took off. Then when I waved good-bye to you. It was tested, but it was never gone."

Julia swiped her tears with the hem of her sweater. "I admire that unwavering faith."

"You have it."

Julia shook her head and took a deep breath. She wasn't ready to talk about the change in her relationship to Chase because she herself hadn't figured it out, but she was finally ready to share something that had tormented her since she'd left. "Cassy, I haven't been back to the cemetery." The moment the words were out of her mouth, her body filled with dread, hating herself for being so weak. She didn't stop speaking; she didn't wait for Cassy to reply.

"What kind of mother abandons her child? I moved away from him. I didn't visit him. Or Michael. I still haven't found it in me to go back there and I've been in Shadow Creek for weeks now."

She looked away from her because she didn't know if she'd be able to handle the disappointment that would surely be on her face. Instead, Cassy stood and rounded the table and pulled her into a hug. "You were the best mother I could have ever hoped for, for my grandson. You were the best wife I could have ever wanted for my son. I don't judge you."

Julia pulled back and looked into her eyes. They were filled with unshed tears.

Cassy gripped her arms. "They aren't there. Their souls are gone, Julia. Don't feel bad for not going. They left this earth with souls filled with your love. Matthew was filled with all the best of you, and with a heart so pure and sweet. You don't need me to tell you that he's in your heart, he's with you in everything you do. I know that already. I see him, in your eyes, in your smile. I see Matthew in you every day. We all had to find our way, and none of it was the wrong way. I believe in you. You're one of the strong ones, Julia. Don't judge yourself. Be proud that you're still standing. Embrace the life you have, be the mother, the woman that Matthew knew."

Guilt poured out of her in a rush and a sob and she hugged Cassy, feeling everything the woman had said to her. She released the guilt.

"Mom, why are you making Julia cry?"

Julia and Cassy turned to see Edward and Gwen standing in the doorway. She found it in her to laugh as Cassy perched her hands on her wide hips. "I'm not. We're having some girl talk."

Julia wiped her tears and focused on the family in front of her. Cassy was already standing and quickly hiding unwrapped gifts as Edward started eyeing the table.

"I'm fine, I'm fine," Julia said as Gwen stared at her. Lola sat by her side, a worried look on the dog's face. Julia patted her head. "I'm fine, Lola." Satisfied, the dog lay down under the table.

"Well, girl talk needs pie. Gwen, why don't you go cut that fresh pecan pie you made today?'

"Dad, you never miss an opportunity, do you? And since when are you the expert on girl talk anyway?"

Edward waved off their teasing and sat down at the head of the table. He eyed some of the gifts again, but Cassy swatted his hand away. "No peeking, Edward."

He grinned mischievously and patted Lola on the head. "I guess you'll have to distract me with pie and a cup of decaf."

Julia laughed, happy to be here, with them. She had missed them all so much. She squeezed Cassy's hand, feeling the warmth from the woman, from her wise words touching her. She knew what she needed to do. She knew she needed to move forward, to take steps in creating a new life. Right now, she was content with making Edward a cup of coffee. "Okay, Gwen, you get Dad the pie and I'll brew the coffee."

Cassy wagged a finger at the two of them. "You two are enablers."

"'Tis the season," Gwen said.

Chapter Twelve

"I can't believe it's moving day already! I've never moved before!"

Maggie was running around the new house, her voice echoing in the empty space. There was only a week and half left before Christmas.

Since spending the night with Chase, she'd seen him and Maggie every day, but they'd both decided they didn't want to confuse or hurt her, so their night together was it...until... neither of them spoke about her leaving after the holidays. They also hadn't talked about everything Chase had revealed to her, but it had changed things. She felt their connection grow deeper and a part of her was terrified of the love she felt for him. Her heart knew the only answer, but her mind hadn't let go of the fear. And since her chat with Cassy, she still hadn't gathered up the courage to go visit Matthew or Michael.

"Auntie Julia, I'm so happy you showed Daddy this house!"

Julia laughed. "It's pretty awesome, isn't it?"

"Yeah! And Daddy said our new furniture is coming tomorrow too."

Julia turned to look at Chase, raising an eyebrow. "You've been shopping?"

He shrugged, as he drilled a screw into the drywall above the window in Maggie's bedroom. He was doing the finishing touches on installing the curtain rod. "I one-clicked the hell out of Pottery Barn."

"Daddy, 'hell' is a swear word. Remember you got me in trouble for saying 'what the hell.'"

"Yup, remember. Thanks for the reminder."

Julia tried not to laugh out loud. Chase was smiling, pride stamped clearly on his handsome face as his daughter tore through the house, dashing from one room to another, squealing with delight.

"I guess she likes it," Julia said, smiling.

"I love it," Maggie screamed from somewhere down the hallway that led to the bedrooms.

They both laughed.

"This place looks spotless."

"The cleaners came in again yesterday, scrubbed it from top to bottom." Chase held out his hand for her coat and she gave it to him. "Painting was finished the day before that."

"Wow, you are a man who knows how to get things done."

He grinned, looking more than a little pleased by her compliment and like he had something he wanted to add to that statement. "I needed this place up and running as quickly as possible or the idea of being in here for Christmas wouldn't be a smart one if we're still living out of boxes."

"Well, I'm here and I've got nothing to do for the next two weeks. I'm all yours." The second those words came out of her mouth, she felt her cheeks burst into flames. It didn't help that Chase was staring at her as though she was a giant piece of cherry pie. Or maybe it was because the man had such presence that he seemed to take up the entire space, wherever he was. "Well, I can think of better ways to spend our time than unpacking."

That slight tilting of his lips at the corner of his mouth added to her suspicions. She was getting in over her head with him. She was struggling with all of this. The idea of leaving filled her with dread and the idea of staying filled her with fear, but she was going to have to make a decision very soon. She was scared she was not what Chase or Maggie needed in their lives. They needed someone strong and without baggage. Maggie needed a mother that didn't come with a broken heart; she needed someone whole. And Chase…he needed a fearless woman, a woman who knew what she wanted, who could be the perfect partner to an already strong man. She could be none of those things to either of them.

"Daddy, when did you have time to paint my room?" Maggie said as she ran into the hallway. Julia was thankful for the interruption.

"I didn't. I had it painted, but it was the color you chose."

"They did a pretty good job."

"Glad you approve, sweetheart."

"When do they start the reno on the kitchen?" Julia asked.

"Right after New Year's," he said, putting his drill back into the toolbox and straightening up to look at her.

"That's great. How did you decide on what you wanted?"

"It was pretty simple. I went into John's Cabinetry on Main Street, and basically told them everything you told me."

She choked. "But I didn't tell you anything."

He shrugged. "It was enough to go on. You know, the banged up cabinetry, the island in a different color, that farmer sink. Then they came out and took the measurements. I approved the drawings and now they're having everything built."

"That is efficient," she said, trying not to let her horror

show over the free range he'd just given the kitchen designer. She took a sip of her takeout coffee that was perched on the window sill.

"Kitchen design isn't really my specialty," he said. "I needed it over and done as fast as possible."

"It's true. Daddy is too busy to deal with this kind of stuff," Maggie said, patting him on the back and looking very serious.

Julia laughed and Chase rolled his eyes. "Maggie, where do you come up with this stuff?"

Maggie shrugged, a mischievous look on her face. "I read between the lines."

Chase shook his head but he was smiling.

"When's our furniture coming?"

"Everything should arrive tomorrow," he said, picking Maggie up and placing her on the counter, her legs dangling.

"I can't wait. I get a new quilt for my bed too, Auntie Julia."

Julia smiled. "That's so great, Maggie."

"Yeah, that Pottery Barn place is great. They had stuff for everyone."

"I had no idea this would be such a hit for you," Julia said, trying not to laugh at him. Just the thought of big, tough Chase ordering from Pottery Barn and Pottery Barn Kids was so endearing.

"Again, I need to be in and out. I was done in two hours."

She choked on her coffee. "You mean you shopped for an entire house in two hours?"

"Is that bad?"

She shook her head slowly. "That's pretty impressive. Usually I hem and haw, put things in my shopping cart, then take them out and add different things. I can never decide."

"Oh. Well, I picked a room I liked from their catalogue and ordered it."

"You ordered *the room*?"

He nodded. "That way I didn't have to worry about it matching or not. They did all the work."

"That's really…efficient."

"That's what I thought, Auntie Julia. I mean, what does Daddy know about decorating? First, I was very worried, but then when he showed me pictures of different living rooms and we picked our favorite, he just added all those things to the order. I was relieved."

This time they all laughed.

"I'm going to finish installing those blinds in my office and the family room," Chase said.

"Why don't we go outside and build a snowman for your front yard, Maggie?"

Maggie jumped off the counter and ran to the front door. "Yes!"

"We'll be outside and hopefully that'll give you some time to get some uninterrupted work done around here," Julia said, aware that they were finally alone. Chase was on the same page because he swallowed up the distance between them in a second, only for Maggie to barrel through the doorway. Somehow the child had managed to get completely ready in full-on snow gear in a minute. "Ready, Auntie Julia?"

Chase ducked his head, rubbing the back of his neck.

Julia smiled. "You bet, sweetie."

• • •

One hour later, Chase tugged on his gloves and stood on the front porch. He didn't announce his presence yet, he couldn't, because the image of his daughter and Julia rolling what had to be the head of the snowman around the yard filled him with something that was becoming more and more familiar since Julia came back to town. He was not used to opening up.

He never did like it. Even his ex-wife had never known him on that level, but Julia had cut through everything. He'd been able to be himself, show her the man he really was.

It was a peace he'd never felt. Something he'd imagined, but never truly experienced. It made him think sappy things, brought a lump to his throat. This is what he wanted. God, how badly did he want this?

The snowball that landed in his face, however, was a cold reminder he had no business wishing for things that would probably never happen. It also reminded him what a badass Julia was when she was at her happiest, the way she used to be. He grinned, walking down the front steps, his eyes on hers. Both women shrieked at his approach and his traitorous daughter yelled out, "Don't worry, his aim is horrible."

He tried not to laugh out loud.

Maggie hid behind the snowman, but Julia kept running. When Maggie turned her head to see where Julia was headed, he quickly dumped a pile of snow on her as he passed. She screamed, promising revenge. He laughed and kept on walking, catching a glimpse of a red scarf trailing through the trees.

He glanced back at Maggie to make sure she wasn't following him. She wasn't; his daughter was currently laughing maniacally and rolling a giant snowball no doubt meant for him, and the minute he turned his head a dense, cold, wet snowball hit him in the back of the head. He whipped around and then ran after Julia, laughing as he heard her laughter trailing behind her. God, was it good to hear her laugh. Seconds later he had caught up to her, grabbed her hand, tugged her over to him, and pinned her lightly against a tree. The laughter stopped immediately as their bodies made contact. Her smile had faltered, but her eyes were a brilliant shade of green, the light of awareness filling them.

"Julia." His voice sounded gruff to his ears. He reached

out to pull the hair that kept blowing in her face.

"Chase, clearly, I'm the better shot."

He grinned, dipping his head slightly. God, how he wished they were alone right now and not in the company of a child that was about to ambush them with snow. He had about sixty seconds. "I'm a gentleman and needed to go easy on you."

"Nice cover," she said, her gaze going from his eyes to his lips in a way that made all his self-control vanish.

"Or maybe I wanted to get you alone. Maybe I haven't been able to sleep since the night in this house. Maybe I can't get you out of my head, and all I can think about is tasting you again, feeling you."

Her lips parted and a smart-ass retort didn't come out. Instead, her hands reached out to grasp the front of his coat. "Then stop talking and kiss me."

That was all the encouragement he needed. His lips hovered close to hers for a moment. And in that moment of almost perfect heaven, his daughter screamed, "Avalanche!"

He pulled back immediately, swallowing all the expletives that were on the tip of his tongue as a bucket full of snow was thrown at him. Julia screamed with laughter as did Maggie. He let out a giant growl and ran toward Maggie, who was barely able to run from him because she was laughing so hard. He grabbed her and tossed her in the air. Seconds later she was begging for mercy and the three of them declared a truce.

They proceeded to create a slightly insane looking snowman that day. 'Mr. Flake' was situated in the center of the front yard, perfectly in the middle of the living room window.

Chase knew he'd look back on this day as one of the most perfect in his life. He didn't care if it made him a sap. Today, his daughter looked as though she'd never been burdened by the pain of a mother leaving her. She looked like a child who was living a happy life, and Julia looked like a woman who'd never known pain either. And that night when they were on their way out to dinner and he caught his reflection in the mirror, he realized that he looked like a man that finally knew the love of a good woman.

Dammit, if that didn't set himself up to be destroyed.

Chapter Thirteen

Chase cursed the chaos that was his life. He was at least a half hour outside of Shadow Creek and he was supposed to pick up Julia in twenty minutes. He loathed being late in general, but being late for Julia was worse. It put him in a foul mood.

He had managed to get the night off and arranged for Maggie to have a sleepover at the Baileys' while he took Julia out. But he had something even better planned than dinner out in public, because he knew neither of them wanted to be out on the town with everyone gawking at them. He wanted to have her all to himself. He wanted a night where they didn't have to worry about anything. Except a late afternoon call landed him out of town and heavy snow was making the drive back impossible.

He increased the speed of the windshield wipers and kept his attention focused on the dark rural road in front of him. He'd get there soon enough. Barely perceptible movement on the side of the road ahead made him slow slightly, not sure if he saw an animal or something. Last thing he needed was to hit a deer on his way to pick up Julia.

He cursed out loud as he realized it wasn't a deer but a toddler. He slowed the car and made a U-turn, not taking his attention off the slow-moving child. He hopped out of the car and immediately started running for the kid when he saw headlights in the distance. His gut churned and he felt a shudder run through him at the sight of the little girl in a T-shirt and boots and nothing else. The weather was frigid, snowing, downright dangerous. He stopped running when he was within a few feet of the child and she finally noticed him.

It was as though someone had punched him in the gut. The little girl's face was dirty, tear-streaked, and gaunt. Her eyes widened as he approached.

"Hi, sweetie. Where's your mom and dad?" he said in his gentlest voice.

Her chin started trembling and Chase looked around. There was a small unplowed driveway that led to a battered-looking ranch house. She didn't say anything so he pointed to the house. "Are they in there?"

After a few seconds of not moving she nodded. He wanted to get her inside and warm. He needed to check out what was happening inside the house. It didn't look good. Yeah, kids wandered off, but this girl was filthy, scared-looking. Kids like this gutted him. He was a kid like this once. A gust of wind blew down hard and she teetered slightly. He needed to hurry up.

"Can I pick you up and carry you back home?" When she still didn't speak, he tried again. He crouched down so they were at eye level. "I've got a nice and warm coat. I bet you're cold, aren't you? I'm here to help you. I'm a sheriff and my job is to help people."

She didn't say anything, but when he reached out to pick her up, she didn't fight him. He wrapped her up in his coat. She was shaking and felt like a block of ice as he carried her. Seconds later her head huddled into the base of his throat and he tried not to pre-judge the situation, but his gut was churning and he was itching to find out what the hell was happening inside the house.

As they approached the entry, angry voices and loud, crashing noises filtered into the open air. The child flinched at each crash. Beer bottles littered the walkway and garbage was strewn about. He sidestepped all of it and made his way up to the front door. He banged on it loudly with his fist and repeated the motion again when no one answered after a few minutes.

Finally, a man with an unkempt beard, a dirty wife-beater shirt and baggy, stained jeans answered the door. His scowl gave Chase a pretty good idea of how this was going to go.

"What the hell you doing with my kid?"

Chase managed to flash his badge without letting go of the little girl. He wasn't about to hand her over in an environment like this. "Sheriff." The man barely flinched. "I found her on the side of the road. She could have been hit by a car. She could have frozen to death."

"She likes to wander off."

"Then get a lock."

"Don't you be telling me how to raise my kid."

"I need you to stand back from the door while I come in."

He cussed but did as asked. Chase walked in, the little girl still huddled into him. It was pretty telling that she didn't even make an attempt to go to her father. The stench of garbage, alcohol, and feces hit him as he entered the filthy home. Stark, powerful images from his past flashed before him and it took everything in him, every ounce of training he'd ever received, not to lose it right then and there. He wanted to take this little girl and bring her as far away from these people as he could. He already knew what he had to do.

He was reaching for his phone when a thin, dark-haired women stumbled into the room. She looked wasted, and judging by the almost empty bottle of gin in her hand, probably was.

"What are you doing with my baby?" she screeched, lunging for him.

He backed up and she staggered forward, falling into a chair. He clenched his teeth, wanting so badly not to be wearing a badge or have a protocol to follow.

"This here's the sheriff, Suzie. 'Parrently, 'yer motherin' skills are lackin.'"

Before he was forced to listen to her retort, Chase spoke. "I found your daughter on the side of the road, freezing, and about to walk onto the road."

The woman's eyes widened. "Well, thanks. Now you can leave her an' be on yer way."

"I'm afraid it isn't that simple now, ma'am." He pulled out his phone with some difficulty since the child was still attached to him and dialed into the station. He would have liked to sit down, but since the place was covered in filth, he'd rather struggle. Seconds later dispatch had him hooked up with the local Child Services department.

Both parents started yelling when they heard his conversation and he moved away from them. The little girl clung tightly to him and he fought down his rage. He never took calling in Child Services lightly. In many circumstances, kids staying with less than ideal parents was still by far better the better choice. But this was the only option.

Looking around him, he knew this place wasn't safe for human inhabitation, especially a child. Pieces of drywall were missing, some were punctured. Half the ceiling in the entry was undone. Then there was the garbage situation. Rodent feces were visible. He knew this home. He knew this home in a way that no one would understand, and he knew these parents. And God, did he loathe this type of parent.

As soon as he was off the phone, the father lunged for

him. Chase sidestepped him. Oh how he wanted to lay his hands on him, but there was no way, not with the little girl. "Sit down beside your wife, or I'll have to use force. If you want a hope in hell of us going easy on you, you'll do as you're told. Understand?"

His wife tugged on his shirt and he reluctantly agreed.

"What's your name, sweetheart?" he whispered in the little girl's ear.

She didn't answer.

The scoff he heard made him straighten her back.

"Her name's Sammy. She don't talk."

It wasn't a surprise. He could list at least five reasons this little girl didn't speak. He ignored them and walked across the room.

"It's going to be okay, Sammy," he whispered, just loud enough that only she could hear. Chase stood at the window, watching cars drive by, holding a little girl he knew very little about. But in some ways he knew more about her than probably her own parents. And she unknowingly knew about him. They were one and the same. Just like any kid or adult being raised in an environment like this. She knew more about him in some ways than even Julia did. He'd never let her in on this part of his life. He'd never told anyone. Julia. God, he was at least two hours late at this point.

He ran his hand over his jaw and shifted Sammy's weight to his other arm. She was light for a child her age. Underweight for sure. She held on to him like she was clinging to a buoy in a storm. Maybe he was. Maybe she'd dreamed of someone finding her, coming in to save her. Half an hour later one of his officers and a familiar social services worker knocked on the door.

He could leave now. He trusted both of them. He tried to let go of Sammy, but she wouldn't budge. Mary, from Social Services, finally managed to cajole her into her arms with a brown bear. He had a lot of respect and trust for Mary. She went above and beyond and was dedicated.

He leaned down to look at Sammy, her scared, wide eyes staring at him. "Sammy, you're going to be okay. I promise you. This nice lady, Mary, is going to take care of you, okay?"

She didn't say anything, just stared at him and clutched the bear. He knew she understood him. "I'm going to check in on you tomorrow. I promise. Do you understand? Do you believe me?"

After a long moment, she nodded. Relief surged through him.

"You're safe, Sammy. You're safe now."

She closed her eyes and tears sprung from her shut lids and streamed down her dirty face. He touched the top of her head gently.

After briefing his officer and Mary, he left. He took a deep breath that to his surprise came out like a shudder, when he left the house. He walked through the blowing snow to his SUV parked on the side of the road, trying to regain his composure. He was able on a daily basis to not think about his parents. He'd also been able to block most of the details about his childhood years.

Yes, he remembered the substance abuse, the filth, the hoarding. But this, what he'd seen today, the little details, they made him remember the other shit. The rodents. The image of a bottle dangling in his mother or father's hand. The smell of his own dirty, filthy body. He stood by the side of his SUV and hurled into the snow. When he was finished he forced his mind to go blank. He squeezed his eyes shut, took a deep breath, and counted backward from ten.

He whipped open the trunk of his SUV and pulled out his overnight bag, searching for mouthwash. He pulled out his phone, cringing when he saw a text from Julia:

Hey, Chase, no worries if you're running late. Just be safe.

He glanced at the time and swore when he realized just how late he was. He didn't want to cancel, but God, he didn't know what kind of company he'd be tonight. It was supposed to have been a special night, but it was ruined now. There was no way he'd be able to shake this off that fast and be the guy Julia was supposed to fall in love with. And there was no way he could tell her any of this without revealing his own past.

He texted back:

Sorry for not texting earlier. Work situation. Be there in thirty mins.

He needed to shower, but he'd pick her up first before he changed his mind.

His stupid past is what he blamed on his lack of attention to his surroundings, to his slow reaction to the sound of rapidly approaching footsteps, to the shout from his officer, and ultimately to the bullet through his left shoulder from behind.

The force of the impact brought him to his knees, but he managed to turn in the direction of the gunfire. His officer was already there, pinning the dad to the ground. Chase managed to call in for help as he slumped to the ground. He watched, numbly, as his blood turned the snow red. He closed his eyes briefly as pain shot through his upper body, images of his daughter and Julia pummeling through his mind. He knew Maggie wouldn't be scared. But Julia…

He leaned his head back against his car tire and shut his eyes, relieved when he heard sirens in the distance. Hell, this was going to send Julia running.

• • •

Julia woke to the wonderful sound of Chase arguing with someone. She opened one eye, careful not to disturb Maggie who was still sleeping, sprawled across Julia on the small couch in the hospital room. Relief and gratitude swept through her at the sight of Chase, sitting up in bed and speaking in a hushed, but frustrated tone with the nurse.

"I'm perfectly fine. There's no reason to keep me in the hospital." His hair was all disheveled, and his dark stubble was a contrast to the pallor of his face. But he was alive. And well. Clearly well enough to hold an argument.

"Sheriff Donovan, they don't let anyone out of the hospital that soon after surgery."

"It was barely surgery."

"It was really surgery, I can assure you," the nurse murmured, a smile on her face as she double checked his chart.

"Can you ask the doctor?"

The nurse sighed but a second later smiled. "I'll see what I can do." She bustled out of the room a moment later. Her heart was heavy in her chest as she watched him, his face slightly pinched with pain, but clearly lucid and healthy after having emergency surgery the night before.

She gently lifted Maggie off her and adjusted her carefully; thankfully the little girl kept sleeping. Julia approached the bed and tried not to humiliate herself by crying, but the moment Chase's blue eyes made contact with hers she had a hard time keeping it together. Last night when the call had come through to the Baileys they had all rushed over to the hospital. She had been strong for Maggie, not wanting the little girl to be even more afraid. But she had removed herself a few times, going into the washroom by herself and splashing cold water on her face.

Her chin wobbled and her eyes blurred with tears as Chase held his good hand out to her. She folded her arms tightly around her body, afraid to go closer, but unable to refuse him. The second her hand made contact with his, he drew her in, holding her fiercely. "I was so scared, Chase," she whispered against his warm neck.

"I know, darling, I know. But I'm fine."

She nodded against him, not wanting to be dramatic, or look like an idiot. The truth was that she didn't know if *she* was fine. She didn't know what this meant—well, she did know; she was falling in love with Chase but she didn't know if she was cut out for this. He lived too close to danger, too close to the edge and she'd promised herself she would never allow herself to feel that kind of loss again.

"Jules, I'm fine. The bullet didn't hit any bone or organs or blood vessels."

"Yup, it must have just gone through a large chunk of fat!" They both turned to find Maggie running up to the bed. They laughed out loud.

"Thanks, baby," Chase said, motioning for Maggie to climb up on the bed. Julia helped her up and her chest hurt as she watched father and daughter cuddle. They looked so alike and Maggie had Chase's resilience.

"When do you get to go home, Daddy?"

"Hopefully today," he said, raising his gaze to Julia's.

"Well, don't rush. Do whatever the doctors tell you to do."

"They want me to stay another night," he said.

Julia crossed her arms. "Then listen to them."

Six hours later, Julia was helping Chase into his bed, despite protests about him being able to do it himself. "You should have listened to the doctor," Julia said as he winced, sitting on the edge of the bed.

"Daddy never listens to anyone," Maggie said with a

theatrical sigh, sitting beside him. Julia stifled her grin. Chase was looking pale but at least he seemed well enough to get around.

"I always listen to you, Maggie," he said, leaning over and giving her a kiss on the head.

"It's time for you to have one of these painkillers," Julia said, taking the bottle out of the paper bag.

"I'm fine, thanks."

Julia crossed her arms and frowned at him. "Chase, don't be difficult. You look pale and clearly in pain."

He shook his head. "Nope, not in pain, see?" He lifted his wounded shoulder then let out a string of curses. "Sorry," he groaned.

"Daddy sometimes uses foul language when he thinks no one is listening, Auntie Julia. You might need to cover your ears."

Julia laughed as Chase shook his head. She pulled out two tablets and handed him a bottled water. "Take these or you'll hear my own foul language."

He managed a devilish grin. "Promises, promises."

"Daddy, Julia is just joking, she has great manners."

"You're right. Why don't you get ready for bed, Maggie? I think it should be an early night for both of us."

Maggie nodded agreeably. "Okay. I'll come in to check on you before I go to bed."

He ruffled her hair. "Please do."

"I need a shower," Chase said once Maggie had left the room. His features were taut as he slowly stood.

"Let me help you," she said, rushing to his side. "Oh and you're not supposed to get your wound wet—"

"Jules. I'm fine. I promise." She felt the sting of his rejection and backed up a step, letting him have his space. He walked away from her and shut the door. Seconds later she heard water running. She sat on the edge of the bed with a shaky sigh. She had no idea what she was doing except none of this felt safe anymore.

She jumped when he walked out of the bathroom ten minutes later. He didn't have a shirt on, and water clung to his wide shoulders. Her gaze went to the taped up shoulder, white gauze a contrast to his darker skin. He was wearing a pair of boxers and didn't seem to mind that she was half drooling and half crying, just watching him cross the room and get into bed.

She walked to stand in front of him. "Chase, are you okay?"

He ran his hand over his jaw, and muscles rippled everywhere with the motion. For a second she thought he was going to dismiss her question, but he didn't. Instead, he reached for her, pulling her close, and buried his head in her neck. She wrapped her arms around him, feeling the tremor that ripped through his hard body. She kissed his shoulder and then pulled back to look up at him. She framed his face with her hands and looked into his eyes, catching a vulnerability in them she'd never seen before.

"This was not the way today was supposed to go," he said harshly.

"I don't care. It doesn't matter. What matters is you're home safe. Why don't you tell me what's bothering you."

He grasped her wrists gently, pulling them away from him. "It's nothing."

She put her hands on her hips. "Okay, well, I'm not stupid. I've known you for how many years? You've never been like this. You think I can't handle it? Only the big, strong Chase is capable of saving people?"

He almost laughed. "How did I forget that you're a ballbreaker?"

His gaze dipped to her shirt, which was currently tightly stretched across her breasts because her hands were still on her hips. "Why don't we find other ways of stress relief? Talking is boring," he said, with a half-grin, looking slightly more like the man she knew.

She laughed and held up her hand. "Nope, not until you spill. Besides, you are injured and only have one arm."

He shrugged. "I'm more than willing to show you what I can do with only one hand."

She rolled her eyes. "Tell me what happened."

He turned his head from her, his profile turning serious. "I'd rather move on from this."

So did she, but she needed to know more. "Chase…"

"Okay. Fine. Found a kid on the side of the road."

He paused when she gasped. She waved her hand. "It's fine, it's fine. I promise. Continue."

He sighed. "She had wandered out of the house. Her deadbeat alcoholic parents were inside. I waited until social services arrived and I knew she would be safe. That's it."

"Oh that's awful. Poor little girl. How old was she?"

He shrugged. "Maybe three. Four. She couldn't speak. She was the sweetest little thing." He whispered that last bit and her heart swelled at the emotion in his voice.

"How were her parents?"

He shook his head. "Drunks. The house was squalor. Rodent crap."

He paused when she gasped again.

"Sorry." She winced.

"She was so skinny. So damn sad and helpless." The man that had always seemed so much larger than life to her was now standing here, vulnerable, and it broke her heart. She wrapped her arms around him and felt him rest his head on top of hers. "Her father chased me and my mind was distracted, I didn't even see him coming when he shot me."

She held on to him tighter and shuddered at how much worse it could have all been.

"It's how I grew up, Julia." She didn't move for a second, wondering if she might have misinterpreted the meaning of what he'd just said. She pulled back and looked up at him. She reached out for his hand and he looked down at it for a moment before finally pulling it free.

"What do you mean?"

His jaw clenched repeatedly. "I was raised by two inept alcoholics, exactly like that little girl. I had to take care of them and myself from the second I was old enough. They were worthless, pathetic people who would have let me die. I left home at fifteen, got a job, went back to high school eventually. The rest is history."

"I'm sorry," she whispered, trying not to cry. She knew he wasn't looking for sympathy. She knew he was watching her for some kind of disgusted reaction or judgment. "Have you seen your parents since?"

He looked toward the window. "No. Pretty bad, right?"

She shook her head and was about to open her mouth, but he started talking again.

"I can't deal with that part of my life, I can't acknowledge what I was. I thought I had come so far, but seeing that little girl, that house, those drunks." He stopped speaking abruptly and ran his hands through his hair roughly. "You want to be an ass, you want to live a certain way, then fine. You lose that right when you have a kid, because now you've screwed up that kid's life, you know?"

She nodded, swiping away the tears that she couldn't help.

"I'd die for Maggie, to keep her safe, to keep her happy. And then I see people like that who are so selfish they can't honor that little girl's life. I think of you, and what you would do to have your little boy alive again. God, sometimes life is so damn unfair." His eyes glistened with tears and his strong chin trembled for a moment. She wrapped her arms around his naked torso and held him close. Seconds later, his arms circled her and she felt his lips on her head. He kissed her hair, then moved to her ear, her cheekbone. She lifted her face to his and looked at him.

There wasn't vulnerability anymore. It had been replaced by a hunger, a desire, for her. And there was something else as he dipped his head and proceeded to make a feast of her mouth. It was the unmistakable look of love. It was new, or maybe it had always been there, but now she wanted it more than ever, even though she was more terrified than ever.

"I need to know that you're going to stay, Jules," he whispered, pulling back and looking at her.

Tears flooded her eyes. "You scared the hell out of me, Chase."

He nodded, his face serious. "I know I did. But I'm fine."

"I keep asking myself if I can do this…if I can live knowing that you are in danger every day you go to work. I don't know how I'd sleep at night if you were working."

"There are no guarantees for any of us, you know that, honey," he said softly, gently.

She nodded. "I know, I know."

"Maggie cried for her mommy and I didn't know what to tell her. When I stayed up with her every single night trying to pry her away from the front window because she'd stand there looking for Sandy and then I'd have to go to work the next morning on no sleep and rely on the Baileys to watch her for me. And then when I had to sleep in her bed for a year, because she was so damn afraid that she'd wake up and I'd be gone too. I promised her I'd always come back."

"I love that about you—I love that you have this unwavering faith that you'll always come home to your little girl."

"And you. I'll always come back to you."

She looked down at her hands, her chest so heavy she found it hard to breathe. This was what she was afraid of. They were too close. All of it was too fast.

"I don't know if I can do this again," she managed to choke out, still not looking at him.

"Do what?"

"Love. Kids. Family. I don't have it in me."

"You do. You just need to try," he said, frustration lining his voice.

She turned to him, guilt seeping through her as he stared at her with a mix of pain and betrayal. "I don't know that I can try."

"You're not going to throw all this away because you're afraid. What you and I have is special. This comes along once in a lifetime, Jules." He fisted a handful of her hair in his hand, gentle but with enough strength to hold her still for a moment, looking into his eyes. "It's always been you. For me, it's always been you. I remember everything, the first time we met, the first time you laughed at something I said or did, the first time we walked home from school together. I remember the conversation we had about Christmas lights—"

"Lights?" she whispered, barely able to keep it together, humbled by what he was telling her.

"You wanted a winter wonderland and I want to give it to you. Don't you dare walk out on us. On me. God, you have no idea how much I love you," he said harshly.

She squeezed her eyes shut and stood, hating herself, but needing space from the intensity of everything he was telling her. "Chase, I can't do this," she finally whispered. "I can't stay in Shadow Creek after the holidays."

His strong jaw was taut. "Fine. You go, figure out what you need to figure out. I'll be here. I don't want to be with you if you don't know you want to be with me and Maggie. I can't have another woman walk out on her."

She didn't say anything, just memorized the way he looked. How handsome he was, wounded, proud, vulnerable. She hated her cowardice.

She hated that she knew she wasn't coming back.

Chapter Fourteen

Julia concentrated on selecting the perfect toy for Maggie, instead of the fact that she had walked out on Chase a few days ago. The charming toy store was exactly as she remembered it and was quite busy which was perfect because it was sometimes easier to get lost in the crowd and she could dwell on her own thoughts.

She knew he wanted her to stay here, start over again in Shadow Creek. A part of her desperately wanted to. She wanted to believe that she could be a family with him and Maggie, that it was the three of them moving into that new house. She wanted to believe that she could heal, start again, and love him with everything she had.

But that would mean she was fearless, and she wasn't. She hadn't been in years. Fear consumed her. She was afraid to love anyone as much as she'd loved Michael and Matthew. When you loved like that, with everything you had, it was too hard to recover if they were taken away. It had ripped her apart. She only wanted to protect herself, to keep love away, to just keep on going. Chase and Maggie had changed that.

The night of the storm she had been terrified he wouldn't come back. She knew, standing in his front window, praying for a glimpse of his headlights, just how much he meant to her. Then when she'd found out he'd been shot...Chase had touched her on so many levels. She had thought she'd be able to leave town after the holidays and be okay. Now she had no idea how she was going to walk away from them. He brought out this other side to her. He brought out a passion she didn't know existed in her, and Maggie brought out the very best of her, just like her little boy had. She was fulfilled with Maggie and Chase.

She picked an armload of gifts and made her way down the aisles to the front cash.

"It's so great to see you again, Julia!"

"You too, Sabrina." She forced a smile on her face as Sabrina, the owner of Jack and Jill's Toy Shoppe, greeted her from behind the old cashier counter. Just a few days ago she had envisioned the three of them on Christmas morning exchanging presents around the tree they'd decorated together. Stupid, sentimental, Julia. Didn't she ever learn? Dreams and wishes were for children, not grown women who'd already learned how cruel life could be. She wanted Maggie and Chase to be happy. In the end, if Maggie's mother was back then she was happy for her. It was her fault for getting hurt. She never should have allowed herself to get so close to them. She never should have allowed herself to fall in love...to spend the night with Chase.

"Is this for Chase's little girl?"

She nodded, slipping on her red wool gloves, and tried to look casual. She knew Sabrina wasn't a gossip. "It is. I hope she likes it."

"I'm sure she will. It's the last one, super popular this year."

"It looks like business is going well?" she asked, trying to change the subject off herself. The charming store had been a fixture in the town for as long she could remember. A visit from Santa usually happened the weekend before Christmas. Julia still loved how small and cozy it was, yet still managed to have a selection of unique and popular gifts.

"It is. I'm trying to keep up with trends, but still trying to incorporate some educational and creative gifts," she said, stuffing some tissue in the red bag. She slid it across the wooden counter. Julia grabbed it by the handle and forced a super cheery grin on her face.

"Well, you've done a great job. It was nice seeing you. Thanks for your help," she said, leaving the store before she ran into someone. She took a deep breath as the blast of cold winter air greeted her upon leaving the little shop. She was only mildly happy to see snow beginning to tumble from the gray sky. Snow reminded her of Chase, and their night together. Well, she was going to have to rid herself of that comparison because she had at least three months of snow ahead of her. She marched down the sidewalk, anxious to turn down one of the side streets before she ran into someone she knew.

"Julia!"

She stopped walking, but took a moment before she forced her feet to move to face the owner of that deep voice. She had tried to get his voice out of her head. All the things he'd whispered…promises, delicious, sweet words she was a fool for thinking she'd ever forget. She clutched the handles of her bag and turned around, and there he was, walking toward her, all confident strides, all delicious, gorgeous Chase. He was in uniform today and she had to quell the flutter in her stomach at the sight of him. She was so hopeless. She commanded herself to not be affected by how he looked, or the warmth and worry in his blue eyes as he finally stood in front of her.

"Are you feeling better?"

"Perfectly fine, see? I'm even cleared for work."

"You were shot. You could have been killed."

His jaw ticked for a moment. "Why are you doing this?"

She fidgeted with the handle on her bag and tried not to look at him as he stood close to her. "What do you mean?"

"I want you to stop running. I want you to choose me and my little girl," he said harshly.

She held up her hand and said the words she'd been avoiding the last few weeks. She hadn't said them in her mind, and certainly not out loud. But if this was the last time they spoke about this before she left town, she needed him to know. "If I weren't, if I were a different person, if there weren't a little girl involved, I'd stay and fight for you. I'd tell you I loved you. I'd tell you that you're the only man that has ever made me feel completely whole. I'd tell you that that night with you was the best night of my life and that I ache for more of you. All of you, for the rest of my life. I'd tell you that being a mom to Maggie is the sweetest, best gift I could have this Christmas. But I can't. We can't."

"Auntie Julia!"

Julia swiped at the tears that had started rolling down her face and backed up a few steps from Chase at the sound of Maggie's voice. He had looked like he'd been about to pull her into his arms and kiss all her common sense from her. She waved as Maggie approached them.

Maggie barrelled into her and her heart squeezed as she hugged her back. "Watcha doing? Are we still going ice skating tonight?"

She stared into Maggie's blue eyes and then looked up at Chase who currently looked as though he'd turned into stone. She searched for something to say that wouldn't make Maggie upset, but Chase beat her to it. "Auntie Julia promised Cassy that she'd stay in tonight. I'll take you. Just me and you."

"I'm sorry sweetheart," she whispered, hating herself.

"It's okay, Auntie Julia. Daddy and I are two peas in a pod, remember? We're used to it just being the two of us!"

She forced a smile and didn't look at Chase. "You all have a great night. I'm going to hurry so that I can get home before dark. Bye!"

Her stomach churned and she felt acid rise in her throat as she walked as fast as she could on the partially snow-covered sidewalks. She needed to leave Shadow Creek as soon as the holidays were over.

Chapter Fifteen

Julia cursed out loud as she landed on her butt, in a pile of snow. Maybe all that pie had gone to the right places, or she'd be even more hurt. She never should have taken Lola on the walk, but after her run-in with Chase and Maggie, she'd needed to burn off some frustration.

She squinted, looking down the street for that damn dog. Lola was going to get a real talking to. Maybe she'd buy the Baileys' dog a gift certificate to obedience school. She brushed the snow off her jeans and slowly stood, a strange familiarity creeping through her body.

She glanced down at the sidewalk. Then up at the black coach light. At the oak tree, at the Japanese maple at the fire hydrant…at her old home. Their old home. The damn dog had led her right onto the street she had vowed never to go down again. The ghosts of her past yanked her out of her safe hiding place and shoved her in front of the reality she had to accept, ruthlessly excavating the memories she'd buried deep inside.

The curtain on her old life rose, and all her memories danced like a meticulously choreographed ballet in front of her: The day they moved in, the day they brought Matthew home from the hospital, the red stroller on the porch, the lawn sign and balloons at his first birthday party, the tricycle on the walkway, the tulips in the spring, the reindeer lawn ornaments at Christmas, the sled and then finally, the *For Sale* sign. When had things gone wrong for Michael? When had she stopped being enough for him?

She shut her eyes for a moment, letting the image in front of her recede, letting the present in, letting Chase's face, his smile, his voice filter through. The memory of Maggie's sweet laugh, the feel of her hand. She opened her eyes again and she knew where she needed to go.

Julia focused on the cloud of cold air as she exhaled, guiding Lola to the place she'd been avoiding for five years. Snow slowly fell in swirling patterns as they walked the quiet residential streets and then the more rural road as they finally came to the outskirts of Shadow Creek.

She stopped walking, her boots crunching against the gravel. Her hand tightened around Lola's leash as she eyed the entrance to the cemetery. She wasn't going to break down.

She knew she needed to come here today. Maybe Lola leading her to her old house was a sign. She needed to confront her guilt, she needed to say good-bye.

"All right, Lola. Ready?"

Lola eyed her for a moment and then gave a bark.

"I'll take that as a yes," she said and the two of them slowly walked down the footpath. The snow had been somewhat cleared but she was glad she'd worn her boots as there were patches of ice and the odd snow drift. She focused her eyes on the towering pines, branches heavy with snow, on the clear blue sky and bright sun. She knew which direction they had to go in and efficiently led Lola down one of the side paths and in a few minutes she found herself standing in a place that felt as though it only existed in her worst dreams. Icy wind blew snow in swirls around them, but it didn't bother her. It was almost as though it didn't matter; it was nothing compared to where she'd been, where she was now.

Lola tugged on the leash and she gave in, walking forward, her boots sinking into the snow. She brushed the snow off the top of Matthew's tombstone and the front of it, revealing the words that Chase had helped her choose, when she hadn't even had the brain power to pick. Her boy's life, summed up in one sentence: *Matthew Bailey, beloved son, grandson, angel.* Julia let herself cry, knowing no one would hear her. She sank to the ground, not caring that her jeans were wet with snow. She was at once one with him; the rest of the world, Lola, everything receding into the background. It was just her and Matthew.

"Matthew, Mama's sorry. I'm so sorry I haven't been back here, but you've been with me every day. In my heart. And I miss you. God how I miss you so much, I ache for you, my sweet baby," she said, her voice coming in a rush of sobs.

"I know Daddy is taking good care of you. I'm okay too." Lola's head nudged her, and then gave her a lick on the side of the face. She peeled off her gloves and traced the engraved letters of his name, barely seeing them through her tears. "I should have brought something for you. I didn't think. I just needed to come here again." She lost track of time as she sat there and talked and cried. This should have been easier; five years was a long time. It wasn't easy. It was one of the hardest things she'd ever done. Sitting here at her son's grave made it all so final, so real. He was gone from this life, her life. God, did she hurt, everything inside of her hurt and brought her right back to that day when she wept at the most incredible, horrifying loss. It was only when Lola started barking at her that she realized the sun was gone, her hands were red and white with cold, and she couldn't feel her feet anymore.

She stood, and turned to Michael's grave. She didn't know

what to say to him because she didn't know the man that had died, so she said the only thing she could. "Good-bye, Michael. Thank you for Matthew. I knew…I knew you did everything to save him. Take care of our baby."

She backed up slowly, careful not to fall and then finally turned, seeking out the path. She waited for the pain to lift, the heaviness, the ache. It did, slowly, but it was replaced by fear as she thought of the people in her life now. She loved Chase and Maggie. She wanted to be Maggie's mom, Chase's wife. She loved Maggie with a maternal instinct and love that she wasn't prepared for. And she loved Chase…in a way she'd never experienced. She wanted them so badly. She wanted a family again — but she didn't know that she could risk it all.

She looked at Michael's tombstone again, giving him a final wave good-bye as Lola tugged on the leash. She couldn't face this kind of pain. She couldn't risk it all again. Wind whipped snow in her face as she stepped through the deep piles. She never should have let herself get close to Chase and Maggie. She wasn't being fair to any of them. She couldn't handle a life of worrying whether or not Chase was safe. The night he was shot had been brutal, sucking her back into the night of the accident. The call that Michael and Matthew had been in a car accident. She couldn't do it again.

She walked away from her baby again, this time strong enough to walk on her own, this time wise enough to not let herself be vulnerable again.

Chapter Sixteen

She was leaving Shadow Creek.

She justified it by telling herself she was being selfless, that she wanted the best for Maggie. But the cold, pathetic truth was that she was running because she was terrified. The kind of terror that had woken her up the last few nights drenched in sweat ever since Chase had been shot.

The next night she'd dreamt Maggie had drowned after the ice broke on the skating pond and she couldn't get to her fast enough, and then she dreamt of her baby. Oh God, she hadn't grown at all, had she? She was so in love with Chase and his little girl and the only way she could deal was by leaving town. She loved him in a way she never thought she could love a man.

Julia clutched the handle on her wheeled suitcase and made her way to the screen mounted on the walls and searched for her bus. The small station was bustling, Christmas travelers being greeted by friends or family, and excited travelers getting ready to leave the town to visit loved ones. This would have been a poignant scene had she not been on her own and running away. There was a man in the corner, playing "The Christmas Song" on his sax, and people dropped bills and coins in his open case.

Something, or someone, made her pause.

She stood motionless in a crowd that was moving and tried to decipher the feeling. A shiver ran through her and her eyes made contact with a man across the station. He was bearded, tall, built, and dressed in cargo pants and a beat up leather jacket. He was scruffy, his hair on the long side…but his eyes. She gasped, and it dawned on her, the exact moment it must have dawned on him. The crowd faded, the noise dimmed, except for the blood rushing in her ears.

It was Jack Bailey. Michael's twin. Her brother-in-law that no one had seen for five years.

She dropped the handle of her suitcase and ran. He met her halfway and then she was being held in his arms. She could feel the tremor that ripped through him. "Jack, you're home. It's so good to see you," she managed to whisper through her tears.

"You too, Jules. How are you?" he asked, pulling back. He looked down at her; they studied each other. They had both run. They hadn't seen each other in years and now they were here, looking at each other as people passed by them, paying them no attention.

"I'm good," she said, swiping at the tears. *Good, except I'm on the run again.*

He frowned slightly. "Why don't I believe you? And why are you leaving on Christmas Eve?"

She closed her eyes. "Long story."

"I've got all night."

She gave a short laugh. "No, you don't. You better get home before your mother loses it. She's planning on cooking the biggest two-day feast ever. You go home, and you surprise them."

"I'm bringing you with me."

She shook her head, wishing she could. "I…can't."

"Why not?"

She groaned and looked down at her boots. "I can't talk about it."

"Ah. So you're running away."

She crossed her arms and looked up at him. It was funny, because she'd wondered about seeing him again, if he would trigger too many memories, if he would be too much like Michael. But Jack had always been his own man, he'd always had an edge to him that made her never truly feel like she knew him, but he'd always been good to her. He'd always treated her like family, and right now, standing here, knowing what she knew about Michael…she didn't see many similarities between them at all.

She pursed her lips and he grinned.

"I know a runner when I see one. I've had to look at myself in the mirror for five years," he said, pointing at his face. "Why would you be running from Shadow Creek right before Christmas? Too painful?" he said, his voice dropping, a tenderness entering.

She could claim it was that and maybe he'd believe her, but she didn't want to lie. Or maybe she secretly wanted his opinion. "It's not that…"

He rolled back on his heels, a slight smile making the corner of his mouth twitch. "Or maybe it has something to do with my good-for-nothing best friend and county sheriff?"

She knew her face was as red as Rudolph's nose and just as obvious.

"So I'm right."

She frowned at him, resisting the urge to stamp her foot. "How did you know?"

Now his grin was full on mischievous. "That idiot has been in love with you since the first day he met you."

Tears flooded her eyes. Oh God, what was she doing walking away from a man like that? "I don't know what I'm doing, Jack. I'm scared, I'm a wimp and I'm running. He was shot last week and I almost lost my mind. I can't do it again."

"You're not a wimp, and I get it. Everything you're saying. What happened to you sucked, sweetheart. I get running. But I'm back here now too and I'm filled with a crap-load of regret and I hurt…people and I don't know if they'll ever forgive me. Don't do it, Jules. Don't be afraid for the rest of your life."

She nodded rapidly but refused to let herself cry. "I love him and Maggie. I want nothing more than to move back here and start a life with them."

"Well, then why the hell don't you?"

Julia froze. It was Chase. She turned around and he was standing there, looking slightly badass and disgruntled, but mostly tender.

Her eyes filled with tears. "What are you doing here?"

He reached out to gently stroke the side of her face and she had to resist the urge to just jump into his arms. "Stopping you. When I said you needed to decide on your own, I wasn't expecting you to actually buy a bus ticket out of town. I came out here as a last-ditch attempt to convince you to stay."

"Nice to see you too, Chase."

Chase grinned, moved forward, and punched Jack on the shoulder. "You too, though you look like crap. Oh and, yes, I was shot, but now I'm fine, thanks for asking."

Jack barked out a laugh. "Thanks and, yeah, you were shot, but I know it'll take more than that to bring you down. So you driving me home?"

Chase handed him his keys. "Wait in the truck. If I don't bring both of you home tonight, Cassy's going to take one of my guns and shoot me. That's a direct quote. We'll be out in a minute. Just don't play with the sirens."

"Funny," Jack mumbled before turning toward the doors.

He paused and looked at her.

"You know you gotta come back with us," he said gruffly. He leaned down and kissed her on the top of her head. "You're family, Jules, come back." He held her stare for a moment and then left.

Julia took a deep breath and looked up at the man that had brought her back from a life without feeling or risk…or love. "Chase—"

"Wait, before you say anything, I want to take you somewhere."

As if she was going to be able to just walk away now. "Where?"

His gaze was intense, his blue eyes trained on her. "Do you trust me?"

"You know I do."

He held out his hand. "Then come with me. We'll drop Jack off and then I'm taking you somewhere. If you still want to leave, I'll drive you back here and you can leave tonight."

Her chest ached at the thought of leaving again. She was so torn. It was easier to leave without saying good-bye, without seeing him. How was she going to leave when being with him felt so right? "Really? You followed me out here, now you're telling me you'll bring me back?"

He shrugged, broad shoulders rising and falling with the motion. There was a mischievous glint in his eyes. "I'm actually banking on you not wanting to leave again, but I'm a man of my word. You want to leave after, I'll bring you back."

It was a step in the right direction. She knew with him was always the right direction.

• • •

Twenty minutes later, Jack had been left on the Baileys' doorstep and they were now pulling into Chase and Maggie's new house.

She knew whatever was happening would impact her deeply. She already knew she loved Chase, but now he was showing her this other side of him, which she already had known existed because he'd shown this kind of patience with his daughter. He was patient, kind. He could have given up on her. He could have been angry that she was trying to leave town without saying good-bye. He could have insulted her or belittled her feelings, but he didn't. Instead he brought her… here. To his new house.

"Come on," he said, getting out of the SUV.

Julia followed him, surprised when he didn't go up to the front porch. Instead, he led them around to the back of the home and up the steps to the deck, and then he left her there while he disappeared somewhere.

Julia stood on the back deck, her boots a foot deep in the packed snow as she stared out into the dark yard. She had no idea where he was. "Chase?"

"Merry Christmas, Julia."

Julia blinked, and then the darkness disappeared, replaced by an almost ethereal light. White lights. Hundreds and hundreds of white, twinkling lights transformed the yard into a paradise where there was no room for darkness. Evergreens, heavy with snow now boasted their gifts of light.

Her voice was trapped somewhere deep inside. This triggered the memory of a walk with Chase when they were young.

Chase appeared at the bottom of the steps, his handsome face shadowed. "Do you remember?"

Julia shook her head and then slowly nodded as the warmth of the memory flooded her body.

"We were seventeen, walking home from school after the play rehearsal. It was dark out and you were giving a running commentary on the Christmas lights in front of each house."

His mouth ventured slightly upward, his eyes unwavering.

Julia swallowed, pushing down the lump in her throat, pushing down the past before it ruined the moment.

"And you said that one day you were going to have your own house and the man you married would be so in love with you that he'd create a winter wonderland of lights for you every year at Christmas."

Julia choked on the sob that broke free and Chase's image blurred with her tears. She remembered. It had been their private memory, a silly teenage dream, one she'd never even told Michael about. But Chase knew. He remembered. That night at his house, she hadn't had time to pull the memory because he'd started kissing her. But he'd been right, he remembered everything about them.

He walked up the remaining steps until he stood still in front of her. Love emanated from him, seeped through her body until she couldn't ignore it anymore. Chase was brave, and strong. And maybe he was invincible.

"Don't leave me, don't leave us, Julia."

She squeezed her eyes shut at the vulnerability in his voice. Chase was never vulnerable. "When I got the call that night you'd been shot I thought I was going to lose my mind and then I saw you there, in that hospital bed." Her voice broke on a sob and he pulled her into his arms, kissing her head.

"I know, I know. But I'm fine. I always come back, remember?"

She pulled back from him slightly. "You can't make that promise. I'm not Maggie."

He frowned. "I'm not leaving you, ever. I'm here."

"I went to see them, Chase," she whispered, her hands grasping his waist.

"Who?"

"Michael and Matthew. I hadn't been back there…since

the funeral."

He leaned forward and kissed her softly. "I would have come with you."

"I know, but I had to do it on my own. I had to say good-bye. And after that I just shut down. All I could think of was you and Maggie and that I loved you both so much and I was just too scared to lose you too. I'm so sorry I walked out, Chase." He wrapped her up in his strong arms and she felt all the worry slowly recede. He made her feel safe, he made her believe everything he said.

"I know, darling. I know. I'm not mad at you, I love you, Jules. I have never needed anyone. I've been the guy to help everyone else get their crap together. I've been dumped on and abandoned and I've grown to accept that that's who I am. I like being strong. I like being dependable. I've learned never to count on anyone else. I'm the only person I can rely on. I don't need anyone. But I need Maggie and I need you, God, how I need you in my life, in my bed, in my soul."

Julia squeezed her eyes shut and tried to find the words to speak but he beat her to it.

"Julia, I have loved you since we were in high school. I have loved you through everything and I swear to God, I would have done anything to spare you the pain of losing Michael and Matthew. But we're here, I'm here, and I'm offering you everything I've got. Me. My little girl. My heart. My soul. You've got me if you want me."

Julia leaned forward, into him, into the man that had saved her five years ago, the man that was saving her now, injecting life and love and faith back into her soul. And the pain of the past was finally less than the pain of not having a future…with Chase.

"God, how could I not want you, Chase? It was never about not wanting you. It was about me." She held his face in front of hers for a moment, letting everything she had come to know about this man play in front of her. The little boy he'd once been, unloved and neglected, to the strong, resilient, brave man he'd become. And he was hers; all she had to do was be as brave as he, and she'd have it all. A family. Motherhood. And a man she loved more than any guarantees of safety, a man she loved more than she ever knew possible.

"You saved me, over and over again. I don't need saving anymore. You've got me. All of me, as whole as I'll ever be. I want to be yours. I want to be Maggie's mama. God, how badly do I want that. I love you both so much, forever," she whispered before his mouth covered hers.

It was the first Christmas in so long that she felt the magic of the season seep through her and fill her with peace and love. Chase had brought her back, he'd given her the gift of love again, the gift of family. She was finally home.

Epilogue

"Happy New Year, Jules," Chase said, grabbing her hand and ushering her into the darkened entryway of the Baileys' home, away from the party. It was just past midnight and Chase kissed her until she could barely stand.

"This was the best New Year's I've had in a long time," she whispered as they slowly pulled apart, the sound of approaching footsteps interrupting their interlude.

"It would have been even better if we were at home, in bed, not at a party."

She laughed at his disgruntled expression. "I don't think there was any way we'd get out of attending this. The Baileys are celebrating Jack's return—what a way for them to start a new year."

Chase kissed the top of her head. "You're right. I haven't seen them this happy in years. But now that it's past midnight, I think we can go. Maggie is already asleep. So we can sneak out and start this new year off right."

"God some things never change." Jack's deep voice, laced with humor made her smile. Chase cursed under his breath and turned around to face his friend.

"When are you going to shave off that god-awful beard? You look like a fugitive."

Jack rubbed his cheek, a lopsided grin on his face. "What are you going to do about it? Do you want my fingerprints?"

"Okay, you two, this is not the time to behave like children. There are more important things to discuss—like have you had a chance to speak with Lily?" Julia whispered.

Jack frowned. "Jules, I'm not going to speak with her."

Her stomach dropped. Her poor friend. "Why not?"

"We can't go back to what we were. She's moved on."

Julia made a mental note of the fact that he said she's moved on...meaning he hadn't. She was going to update Lily tomorrow. "Nothing's ever too late. You should at least speak to her," she said, nudging her chin in the direction of her friend who was currently standing alone and filling up another glass of champagne.

"I'd suggest shaving first," Chase said.

She poked him in the ribs.

"Well, thanks for the advice," Jack said, taking a step away and raising his empty glass of champagne to them.

Julia cringed as she turned around to face Chase again. "I feel so bad for him. He's still not himself."

Chase gave a nod. "I know. Give him time. He came home and did the right thing. He'll get there." His gaze darted from hers. "Oh man, don't look now, he's approaching Lily."

Julia whipped her head around.

"I said don't look," he said, laughter in his voice as they both watched the scene unfold.

Julia held her breath as they watched Jack say something to Lily and hold up his empty glass. Vulnerability was stamped across his handsome face. Lily's expression didn't change, didn't soften at all at whatever he said. Julia's heart started hammering as she watched her dear, sweet friend, lift the bottle of champagne and slowly pour it in Jack's glass. It looked like she was saying something too. And it looked as though she kept on talking, as she kept filling the glass, as champagne started overflowing and she kept pouring.

"Oh hell, that's not going well," Chase said in a strangled voice.

Julia held her breath. Clearly, Lily wasn't ready to start the year off with forgiveness.

They watched, not moving as Jack just stood there as Lily stuffed maraschino cherries in his glass, her eyes narrowed and her mouth moving a mile a minute. "Do you think she's insane?" Chase asked.

Julia stifled a laugh, because none of it was funny at all. "No, she's just really, really mad at him."

Lily stormed off and Jack stood there, champagne, and cherries dripping from his glass and onto his feet. Gwen raced across the room and followed Lily. Jack turned to them and gave them a salute before walking out the patio doors. Alone.

"That was so bad," Julia whispered. "You should go talk to him."

"Guys don't like talking after they've just been humiliated by a woman. Maybe I'll pass by and see him tomorrow," he said, yanking their coats out of the closet. "I think this might be a good time for us to leave."

She slipped on her coat. "I guess."

"Don't let that ruin our night," he said, giving her a kiss.

She smiled up at him. It had taken forever to get to this good place. "I won't. We'll figure out a way to get them back together tomorrow."

"Uh, that's not exactly what I meant."

She patted his shoulder. "That's okay. I'll help you."

He laughed, pulling her out onto the porch. Snowflakes were falling and the air was crisp and tinged with the smell of cedar. He started down the steps and she called out to him, ready to share with him something she'd never thought she'd say again.

"What is it, Jules?" He stood there, on the bottom step, his dark hair sprinkled with white snow. His handsome features were relaxed and happy.

Her eyes filled with tears and a rush of hope and slight fear filled her as she spoke from her heart. "I…if you want…"

He frowned, moving closer to her, taking her hand. "What is it?"

"Have you ever thought about becoming a dad again?"

His blue eyes softened, and her heart swelled when she saw them fill with moisture. "I have." His voice was thick, rough with emotion. "I didn't want to push, or pressure you."

She nodded rapidly, taking a step closer to him. "I want babies with you, Chase."

He closed his eyes for a second and then leaned forward, cupping her face with his hands. "I want to give you babies, Jules. I want to give you everything," he whispered before kissing her. They stood there, wrapped in each other's arms and snow fell around them. Julia knew she was ready for a new year, a new life, with the man holding her.

About the Author

Victoria James is a romance writer living near Toronto. She is a mother to two young children, one very disorderly feline, and wife to her very own hero.

Victoria attended Queen's University and graduated with a degree in English Literature. She then earned a degree in Interior Design. After the birth of her first child she began pursuing her life-long passion of writing.

Her dream of being a published romance author was realized by Entangled in 2012. Victoria is living her dream—staying home with her children and conjuring up happy endings for her characters.

Victoria would love to hear from her readers! Sign up for Victoria's Newsletter and receive a FREE novella by Victoria James! You can visit her at www.victoriajames.ca or Twitter @ vicjames101 or send her an email at Victoria@victoriajames.ca.

Find your Bliss with these great releases...

Snowbound with Mr. Wrong
a novel by Barbara White Daille

Worst. Day. Ever. After Lyssa Barnett's sister tricks her into reprising her role at Snowflake Valley's annual children's party, she doesn't think anything can be worse than squeezing into her too-small elf costume. Then tall, dark, and way too handsome Nick Tavlock shows up to play Santa...and an unexpected storm leaves them snowbound in the isolated lodge. Now Lyssa is trapped with the man who drives her crazy in more than one way. She needs to stay strong—and far way from the mistletoe. Or maybe she just needs a little Christmas spirit...

Her Unexpected Engagement
a *Checkerberry Inn* novel by Kyra Jacobs

Stephanie Fitzpatrick wanted out of the spotlight after her pro-golfer husband was caught on camera cheating. But when a fib told by her well-meaning sister has her looking for a temporary fiancé, she goes to the one man who can help—her former best friend. Before long, the temptation to change the "temporary" arrangement into something more is hard to ignore.

Saving the Sheriff
a *Three River Ranch* novel by Roxanne Snopek

Every year, free-spirited Frankie Sylva banishes her holiday loneliness with good deeds. This time, she's rescuing a truckload of neglected reindeer—until a blizzard sidetracks her scheme. When local sheriff Red LeClair finds her half-frozen and trespassing on Three River Ranch, he has no choice but to take her back to the ranch and keep an eye on her. But when the power goes out, Red and Frankie are forced to depend on each other in a way that both have avoided for years. Will Red be the one Frankie rescues this holiday?

Resisting the Hero
an *Accidentally in Love* novel by Cindi Madsen

When his best friend's sister moves to town, local cop Connor Maguire knows he's in trouble. Faith is feisty, funny, and talks trash like nobody's business. She's also his partner's sister—and so totally off limits. Faith Fitzpatrick isn't looking for a hero. She wants safe, and there's nothing safe about Connor. Confident, sexy, and sporting a six-pack that should be illegal, he's everything she doesn't want. The more time Connor spends with Faith, the more he's willing to risk the wrath of her brother. If he could only convince her to take a risk on him, too.

Made in United States
North Haven, CT
14 April 2023

35442841R00109